IMMINENT PERIL

MELISSA F. MILLER

BROWN STREET BOOKS

1

To say that Dr. Prachi Agarwal was nervous and confused would be to vastly understate the situation. She was an utter and absolute wreck.

Nothing during her short time as an employee of Playtime Toys had prepared her for an impromptu meeting with Charles Merriman, the company's CEO, and Peter Jefferson, the Executive Vice President of Product Innovation. Yet, here she was, in Mr. Merriman's private office, blinking furiously and hoping she wasn't about to be fired.

"Dr. Agarwal, the reason we asked you to join us is that we've got a bit of a situation. It involves the database you're creating," Peter Jefferson began.

She shifted in the leather chair and nodded.

The CEO chimed in, stating the obvious as though it were news. "We sponsored your visa and brought you over here from Bangalore to create and populate a database to track all our products through the development, testing, sales, and marketing life cycle."

"Yes, sir." She thought, not for the first time, that it was astonishing the company had limped along without a functioning database for as long as it had. The creation of a database that suited their needs was complex, due to the way the company seemed to categorize and recategorize products periodically, but it was long overdue. Until now, they'd been using a rudimentary spreadsheet someone's kid had created while home from college on a break.

"And while you know that time is of the essence in your work, you may not know why," Mr. Merriman continued.

Prachi thought. "I understand that another company has made an offer to buy you—to buy us, rather. Mr. Jefferson has mentioned that my work must be completed as part of the sale."

"That's close, but not quite right," Jefferson interjected. "Recreation Group has made an offer to purchase the company and we've agreed to the terms. We have a closing date, but that's not the deadline for your work to be completed."

"It's not?"

He cleared his throat. "No. You see, we were perhaps a bit overzealous and, well, we led the purchasers to believe that we already had a robust database."

"You lied?" The words were out of her mouth before she could stop them.

Mr. Merriman and Mr. Jefferson exchanged dark looks.

"We overstated," Mr. Merriman corrected her. "It was an error, to be sure. And now we're paying for it, aren't we, Peter?"

Mr. Jefferson smiled grimly. "We are indeed. What happened, Dr. Agarwal, is that Recreation Group's lawyers have filed an arbitration claim. They say that the purchase price included some hefty amount for the database, which they now understand is not completed. They're asking the arbitrators to reduce the value of the company."

"I see," she said, even though she didn't see at all.

"The arbitration hearing is scheduled to occur

before the closing date of the transaction," Mr. Merriman told her.

"We need one of two things to happen—we need to have a completed database in Recreation Group's hands before that hearing date or we need to delay the hearing until after the closing."

"Why?" she asked, mystified.

"If we give them the database, the issue goes away. There's no hearing, and the forty-million-dollar purchase price remains. If we can't meet that deadline, we need to push the hearing date back. That way, the sale will still go through at the agreed price. Then, if we don't provide the database, the arbitration panel will determine how much money we need to return to the buyers. Do you understand?"

"Not really," she said. "What difference does it make if the arbitration panel reduces the purchase price before the sale goes through or if it tells you to refund Recreation Group after the fact?" It was the same ultimate result, she thought to herself.

Mr. Merriman gave Mr. Jefferson a meaningful look. "Can you field this one, Peter?"

He nodded. "Simply put, Dr. Agarwal, it doesn't matter to the company. It matters a great deal to

Mr. Merriman and to me, as our buy-out compensation is based on the purchase price."

Ah, of course. Money out of their pockets. The high-level interest in her mundane work suddenly made sense.

"Oh," she said.

"Now, we don't want to hold your feet to the fire. And we know the delays in getting your visa approved ate up a good amount of time. But, we need to know, can you get the database done within the next two weeks?"

She hesitated. Her instinct was to please her superiors and assure them that, yes, of course she could. But the timeline was really very tight—close to impossible. She remembered something her thesis advisor had told her when she was defending her thesis: *Always, always underpromise and overdeliver.*

She squared her shoulders and met the CEO's eyes. "I'm afraid I can't promise that. I'll work as quickly as I can, but you should make a contingency plan."

Mr. Jefferson nodded and spoke in a mournful voice, "We appreciate your honesty, Dr. Agarwal. Please do your best."

"Of course," she promised.

"That'll be all," Mr. Merriman said, dismissing her.

She bobbed her head and scurried out of the room. She closed the door behind her and stood there for a moment, waiting for her heart rate to return to normal. As she did, she heard Mr. Jefferson's voice.

"If we don't get them that blasted database before the hearing date, it all comes crashing down. And, you know, there *is* no contingency plan. We'll have to figure out a way to manufacture a delay, Charles."

"I know a guy."

2

The crisis management consultant locked eyes with his newest client and held his gaze for a moment before answering. He wanted to ensure that he communicated both his understanding of the situation and his commitment to correct it.

In his ideal world, he'd be an inside man, working solely for the company, and their trust in him and his loyalty to them would be beyond question. But this was the twenty-first century: the age of outsourcing; independent contracting; and the gig economy. Most companies either wouldn't —or couldn't—afford to keep someone like him on the payroll full-time, so he'd become a consultant of sorts, one whose services came with a hefty price tag.

His name was passed along on golf courses, on fishing charters, in health club saunas, or over cigars and bourbon in the private rooms of country clubs. One CEO would bemoan a particularly thorny problem and somebody would say, 'Call my guy. He can fix it.' And then his phone would ring. That was how Charles Merriman, the nervous CEO of a successful toy company, had come to find him. He appraised Merriman now—the man was jumpy, almost frantic.

After waiting the appropriate amount of time, he spoke. "I understand what you need, Charles. I'll take care of it."

"But you don't know the details—the timing of the transaction is critical. Are you sure you can help us? The issue is complicated. The lawyers and the bean counters can't even agree on how much it might cost if we can't make it go away."

"I don't need to know every detail. I just need to know the problem. You've told me your problem; now I'll fix it. I fix problems." He said it with authority.

That's what he considered himself after all—a

fixer. The men, and they were almost always men, who required his services preferred to think he was a problem-solver. And despite Merriman's insistence that his problem was unusually complex, it wasn't. Once he'd cut through all the corporate buzzwords and legalese, the consultant understood that the company needed to buy time. And he had figured out a way to make that happen. It wouldn't be easy, but it was simple—elegant even.

Merriman remained unconvinced. He furrowed his brow, anxiety pinging off his body. "How? What will you do?"

He barked out a short laugh. "What I'll do is get you your money. Because that's how I'll get my money. Consider it handled."

Most, but not all, of the tension drained from the CEO's face. A sliver of apprehension remained —the amorphous worry of giving up control. That was the trade-off his clients had to live with. It was a small price to pay, really.

Merriman opened his mouth then closed it, like a big, stupid fish.

"Arrange for the wire," the fixer instructed. He stood and extended his hand.

Merriman examined it for a moment. Then he

squared his shoulders and managed the handshake.

The consultant walked away from a pair of leather chairs nestled against a two-top in the corner of the generic hotel bar and melted into the flow of foot traffic hurrying through the gleaming lobby. The CEO sat alone, staring into his martini glass.

3

Sasha McCandless noticed the man before she even entered the bar. He was sitting with his back to the plate-glass window, his bar stool pulled over a little too close to a cluster of women in their early twenties. Their body language sent an unmistakable 'get lost' message, but he either didn't notice or didn't care.

She eyed him as she walked through the entrance and into the narrow, crowded room. Mid-forties at the youngest; late fifties at the oldest. Salt-and-pepper hair, cut close to his head. Thick neck and broad shoulders, which were straining the seams of his navy suit jacket. The jacket was shiny with age.

She flicked her eyes away and then back to the

women jammed between his barstool and the chalkboard listing the happy hour specials. There were three. Two leggy redheads who could pass for sisters and a petite dark-skinned woman, no taller than Sasha. The small woman and one of the redheads were shooting daggers at the guy. The other redhead had her back to the man—and Sasha—and she was swaying in her heels. The man's hand hovered near the small of her back but didn't make contact.

It's none of your business.

She looked away and focused her attention on pressing through the crowd to find Maisy. Her bright blonde curls made her easy to spot. Sasha stretched up on her tiptoes and scanned the bar. No Maisy. But she did see a couple at the bar settling their tab. As the woman eased herself off her barstool and took her date's arm, Sasha weaved through a knot of business casual polo shirts and khakis and claimed the stools the couple were vacating. She propped her bag on one stool and positioned herself on the other so she could see the door from her peripheral vision, more out of ingrained habit than any need to watch for Maisy.

The bartender picked up the departing

couple's credit card slip and wiped his bar towel across the surface in front of her in a half-hearted circle. "What can I get you? Specials are up there." He pointed to the board behind the redhead.

The happy hour cocktail menu might have appealed to a younger, childless Sasha. But the current, always-exhausted, working-mother-of-twins Sasha knew she'd be facedown on the bar after about half a mixed drink.

"I'll have your house Sangiovese. And a glass of water."

"Do you want a half-carafe or just a glass?"

"Just a glass, please."

He nodded.

From behind her, a familiar, honey-laced voice breathed, "Nonsense. She'll have the half-carafe. And I'll have that gin and basil shrub drink. You know, the one with the lime?"

"The General's Mistress?"

"That's the one," Maisy confirmed as she slid onto the barstool next to Sasha. "Glass of wine, my sweet behind," she murmured as the bartender turned to get their drinks.

Sasha laughed. "Hello to you, too."

Maisy leaned in for a quick half-hug. "Well, I'm

sorry, sugar, but really. How long's it been since we've had a girl's night out?"

Sasha searched her memory but couldn't quite pinpoint the last time she'd seen her old neighbor. "Too long."

"Mmm-hmm. Exactly. So one glass of wine's not going to cut it. Now, how the heck did you manage to stop working at a decent hour for once? Did your office catch fire?"

"I had a close of business filing deadline in a commercial arbitration. I finished up early this afternoon. Then I decided I could catch up on paperwork or meet my favorite journalist for a drink. I'm glad you weren't busy emceeing a gala or something."

Maisy could pretend all she wanted that Sasha's schedule was the only impediment to their socializing, but as one of Pittsburgh's most beloved local news personalities, Maisy spent most of her time in front of a camera or behind a dais at some community event.

"You did have good timing. I'm just finishing up a three-part story about the dangers of shopping at those big consignment sales, you know the ones for kids' clothes and toys?"

Oh, she knew the ones. Most of the women in

her mothers of twins group swore by consignment sales. As she was learning, kids grow fast—and keeping two of them supplied with clothes that fit and age-appropriate toys could strain a budget. She hadn't yet delved into the world of consignment buying or selling, though, because, in her case, time was the scarcest resource. She'd rather pay full price, click a button, and have her well-researched purchases arrive within two days through the magic of free shipping than comb through racks of outgrown clothes and boxes of discarded toys hoping to stumble across a gem.

"Sure. What's the angle? Germs, I bet. Are those used toys so germy?"

"Probably, but that's not what the story's about. Locally, several kids have been injured—or worse—by baby equipment and toys that have been recalled but never removed from the resale market. Apparently, recalls are really common among baby toys and gear."

Sasha nodded grimly. "Small parts, loose straps, collapsing rails, lead paint, beads, batteries. The nursery section of any store is a veritable death trap of potential strangulation, suffocation, and swallowing hazards."

"You make parenting sound like such a

fantastic adventure," Maisy deadpanned. Then she asked, "So is the arbitration thing interesting?"

"I guess that depends on your interests. It's a dispute arising out of a proposed acquisition. We represent a local company that's made an offer to purchase a competitor. But there's an issue about the valuation of one of the intangible assets, and the parties want to arbitrate now rather than after the sale closes."

Maisy's eyes were glazing over. "Got it."

Sasha sipped her wine. "Don't worry, I won't bore you with the details." Unlike criminal defense attorneys, who had loads of entertaining war stories, a corporate litigator was rarely tempted to spin yarns over drinks. The hard truth was nobody was all that interested in the possible breach of an intangible asset provision of a sale and purchase agreement—not even her.

But Maisy cocked her head. "Your firm's not handling the transaction, though, are you?"

"Funny you should ask. Will and I always assumed Naya would want to be a litigator, too. I mean, she was a trial team paralegal before law school. She's got loads of experience, but apparently her heart's desire is to be a mergers and

acquisitions attorney. To each her own, I guess."
She shrugged.

"So Naya's handling the deal?"

"Yes. She brought in the client. She's jazzed to
have the chance to do what she loves. And, frankly,
if she can build a practice, it would be great for the
firm long-term as we grow."

"I don't doubt for a second that Naya can make
a name for herself as a transactional attorney.
You'd better just hope she doesn't angle for top
billing when you make her a partner," Maisy said
with a giggle.

"I don't know. Andrews, McCandless, and
Volmer doesn't sound half bad."

Just then, Maisy's pointy elbow jabbed in
Sasha's side, digging into the soft spot just above
her ribs.

"Ow!"

Maisy jerked her head toward the front corner
of the bar. "Check out that creep."

Sasha followed her gaze. The big guy was
getting bolder. One hand was pressed on the small
of the seated redhead's back and the other
caressed her neck. Even as drunk as she seemed to
be, she wasn't responding. She sat stiffly. Her sister
—or whoever the second redhead was—yanked

her hand and pulled her off the stool. The third woman shot the man a dirty look and moved to stand between him and his target.

"You missed it. He tried to grab her butt a minute ago," Maisy said in a low voice.

"Doesn't this place have bouncers?" Sasha asked. She turned her head to survey the room.

It was sufficiently crowded and noisy that it was entirely possible that the drama playing out in the front corner had gone unnoticed by management. The bartender was at the far end of the bar, ringing up bills, opening beers, and mixing cocktails in a whirl of constant motion. The men in khakis were deep in a discussion about the Penguins' new goalie and either oblivious to, or pretending to be oblivious to, the drama playing out just twenty feet away. Nobody was paying attention to the unfolding sexual assault.

She exhaled and slid off her barstool.

"Nooo," Maisy breathed. "We should stay out of this."

"Would you want someone to help if it were you?"

Maisy sighed. Her eyes slid around the room, desperately looking for someone else who might step into the role of Good Samaritan.

"Her friends are there," she pointed out half-heartedly.

"I'm just going to nicely ask him to back off," Sasha assured her. "You can wait here."

"Oh, no, you don't." Maisy drained her glass and hopped to the ground beside her. "I'm coming with you." As they snaked their way through the crowd, Sasha murmured to Maisy, "When we get there you talk to the girls and see if you can get them away from him. I'll take care of him."

"You won't get any argument from me about that division of labor."

Sasha smiled to herself. Then she cleared her mind and concentrated on her surroundings until the man and the three women came into the foreground in rich, sharply drawn detail and all the noise and activity of the bar around her receded into a soft blur. Her Krav Maga instructor Daniel called this state laser focus.

As she and Maisy drew closer to the small group, the more sober of the two redheads—the one who was not on the receiving end of the man's creepy attention—threw them a desperate look. Sasha smiled and nodded in an effort to reassure the woman that they were coming to help. The redhead nodded back, and relief flooded the dark-skinned brunette's face. The change in their demeanor must have registered with the creep, because he swiveled around on his barstool and gave Sasha a hard, challenging look.

Great. She would have liked to have done this the easy way, but one look at his steely expression made it clear that the hard way would have to do. Still, she hoped against hope that he'd choose to walk away.

"Do you need something?" he said in a brusque tone.

Maisy swooped in and hustled the three women out of the corner. The sober redhead and the brunette went eagerly; the drunk redhead asked loud, confused questions, but she allowed her friends to lead her away. Sasha waited until they'd rounded the corner to answer.

"I do need something. I need you to leave those girls alone," she said in a pleasant, businesslike voice.

He pushed himself to standing and balled his fists. He stared down at her. He had nine, maybe ten, inches and seventy or eighty pounds on her.

"Who the hell are you, the bar mom?"

"That's right. I'm the bar mom. It's time for you to go."

He grabbed his beer, took a long swig, and slammed the empty bottle down on the bar. "Listen, lady, you need to mind your own business. I was just giving those gals some attention."

She smiled tightly. "Your attention isn't welcome. Those women are trying to be polite and give you the brushoff without making a big scene. But since you don't seem to be getting the hint, I'm going to make it easy for you. Leave them alone."

"Or what?" he sneered.

"You don't want to do this. Trust me."

He looked her up and down. Then he laughed. "Am I supposed to be afraid of you?"

"No, of course not."

He nodded.

She went on, "If you were smart, you would be. But you don't look very smart, so no, I don't expect you are."

His face tightened as he stepped forward. From the angle of his arm, he was planning to push her back against the window. If he did, she'd be pinned—not a great fighting position. She planted her feet and waited for his shoulder to move forward. She shot out her left hand and grabbed his right wrist, bending it back. She used his momentum to twist herself so that they were standing side by side. Then she pulled his wrist close to her body and locked it against her right arm.

If she were a regular-sized person, this was the part where she would've hissed in his ear. But her mouth was about level with his throat, so instead, she craned her neck up and looked over at him.

"Now, listen carefully. I could break your wrist right now. It would take almost no effort." She applied just a tiny bit of extra pressure to his wrist to drive home the point. He winced. She went on, talking through her clenched teeth, "But I'm not going to. I'm going to let go of your arm. And you're going to get your stuff and get lost before I change my mind. Any questions?"

The disbelief that had filled his eyes when she grabbed him faded, and a look of embarrassment took its place. "No, no questions."

"Good. Next time you're inspired to chat up a woman at a bar, you should remember your manners. You never know when there's going to be a bar mom around."

She released his hand and stepped back but kept her eyes locked on his. He mumbled something she couldn't make out and grabbed his overcoat from the back of his stool. He shrugged his arms into it and stood with a dejected slump in his shoulders, his arms hanging by his sides.

She realized later, when she was reviewing where it had all gone wrong, that it was his posture of defeat that had lulled her into making her critical mistake. She turned her back on him, intending to join Maisy, who was now rubbing the shoulders of the drunk redhead.

As she stepped away, her eyes drifted up to the long mirror that hung on the wall opposite the bar. Behind her, she saw movement. The man had reached back for his empty beer bottle and had his arm cocked, ready to bring the bottle down on the back of her skull.

She whipped around and drove her open left hand into his nose in a single, fluid motion. He staggered and backed into the bar rail. She allowed her forward momentum to carry her toward him and landed a solid punch in the soft area just below his nose and above his upper lip. His nose was already gushing blood from the palm strike. He wiped it away with his left hand then covered his face. She kept her fists up and watched his face.

He emitted an animalistic howl and lowered his head, charging her as if he were a bull. When the distance was just right, she raised her leg, chambered her knee, and whipped her leg out and up, driving her heel into the underside of his chin. As his head snapped back, she lunged forward and grabbed two fistfuls of his jacket in her hands. He sagged against the bar, breathing hard and bleeding freely, and stared at her with a look of sheer hate.

"Had enough?" she asked as she wondered where the hell the bouncers were. He didn't answer but just kept glaring at her.

Better safe than sorry, she decided. She pulled back her left fist and punched him in the solar plexus. He doubled over with a gasp-grunt.

Suddenly, a cluster of bouncers rushed toward them. A clean-cut, college-age guy in a short-sleeved polo shirt separated them.

He ushered Sasha to a nearby seat. "Are you okay, ma'am?" he asked in a soft, concerned voice.

"I'll be fine." She examined her knuckles but saw no cuts. She'd probably have a few bruises in the morning. She glanced over at her attacker, who was flanked by two more polo-wearing bouncers who loomed over him. "But he's probably going to need stitches," she said in a steady voice.

"You think?" he answered drily.

The creep caught her eye and started shouting.

"I want to press charges," he sputtered, pointing at her. "That bitch is crazy."

She allowed the adrenaline to continue to drain from her body, refusing to let him to amp her back up. "I was defending myself," she explained.

The bouncer gave her a worried look. "I'm really sorry, lady, but it's establishment policy to call the cops whenever there's a bar fight. They're already on their way. You're gonna have to tell them your side of the story and let them sort it out. Are you sure you're okay?"

"I'm sure. I'm also sure the responding officer will understand what happened here once he or she takes our statements." She smiled in an effort to reassure the poor guy. His distress was written all over his face.

"Well, if you're positive you're not hurt. Can I get you anything? A glass of water?"

"A glass of water would be great," she said as she saw the police cruiser come to a stop just outside the door, lights flashing.

4

Prachi bit her lower lip and ran a finger along the row of values. They couldn't possibly be right. She flipped the page to the summary of testing data and scanned the columns. There it was, the mercury content with the same impossible number. Beside it, the analysis: *Outside accepted tolerances.*

She stared at the numbers until her eyes blurred and the numbers swam into one another. Then she rifled through the stack of reports piled almost as high as her cubicle's half-wall and found the heavy metals test results from a previous batch of product. She paged through the report, sheet by sheet, until she found the same data from the earlier batch. The number was significantly lower. *Within normal limits.*

That, frankly, was what she'd expected to find. When Playtime Toys had sponsored her for her H-1B skilled worker visa, they'd been desperate to find someone like her—someone with a dual background in chemistry, to understand and interpret the reams of third-party testing data they were required to obtain on their products, and proficiency in computer programming, to build and manage the database that would house the results, along with all the other information about the products.

During the time it had taken for the government to process her visa, the testing results had simply piled up. Stacks and stacks of unread, in some cases, unopened, reports lined the walls of her office pending her arrival. After she finally arrived in Pennsylvania, the stacks grew higher still while she began the necessary work of coding the database. Then she had to sort the documents into a semblance of order; apparently, as the reports had come in, they'd been tossed aside. The company's focus was on manufacturing the products and pushing them out the door. Nobody had cared about organization, documentation, or process. So now she was facing a mountainous backlog of reports that needed to be entered into the system she'd created.

Even after her meeting with Mr. Merriman and Mr. Jefferson, where they'd been very clear that completing the database was a crucial priority, the human resources department still hadn't responded to her request for help—even a temporary employee or an intern would be a blessing. But as it stood, she was tackling the mountain alone.

Because she was doing all of the input herself, she was certain that none of the other samples entered into her database had been outside normal limits. The third-party testing company that handled the heavy metals testing performed tests weekly. Without fail, every Tuesday, she received a package of testing results. She'd been working backward, in reverse chronological order, to input the most recent tests first. She eyed her piles. The older heavy metals testing results were all grouped together waiting to be entered into the system. There looked to be three dozen or so.

She sucked in a breath. Mr. Merriman and Mr. Jefferson had been crystal clear that clearing the backlog and getting the database up and running was her most critical task. But she couldn't ignore the data. Best practices required her to stop the data entry and double-check the results internally before reaching out to the testing company. She didn't even know where the on-site laboratories were located, let alone how to get the testing underway.

She saved her work in the database, scooped up the testing results, and headed through the maze of cubicles toward the elevator. This problem, as the Americans liked to say, was above her pay grade.

Prachi rapped on the door. Then she stood with her hands clasped in front of her, gripping the report, until she heard Mr. Jefferson's voice.

"Come in."

She pushed the door open and smiled hesitantly. "Sorry to bother you."

"Dr. Agarwal, can I help you with something?"

She stepped all the way into the room. "Yes. I need to talk to you about some testing results."

He frowned. "Hasn't personnel gotten back to you about your request? I'm afraid there's simply no room in the budget to give you an assistant. It's futile to try to plead your case to me. Trust me, if I could've authorized the expense, I would have. But we're under a 'no new expenditures' order until the sale of the company, direct from the Chief Financial Officer."

"That's not why I'm here."

"Oh?" He swiveled in his desk chair to face her.

"The heavy metal testing results for the most recent batch of product AR462 are ... well ... they're unusual."

"AR462," he mumbled to himself as though he were searching a mental list. "In what way are they unusual?"

"The sample exceeds the tolerances for organic mercury."

"Mercury?"

"Yes," she confirmed. "The other substances were all within normal limits. I went back to the results for the previous batch. That sample was completely within limits, including the mercury. Has the manufacturing process changed in some way?"

"No."

"I thought not. So, obviously, we need to retest the samples in-house. How do I arrange for that?"

He looked at her in disbelief for several seconds before managing a response. "Dr. Agarwal, did you not understand what Mr. Merriman and I told you? You focus on finishing the data-base. Pronto."

She tried not to react, but she bristled at his tone. Yes, she understood they needed to have a functioning database before the sale went through so that they could become multimillionaires instead of regular old millionaires, but this was a safety issue.

Perhaps *he* hadn't understood *her*. She tried again, "The mercury levels are dangerously high, and this product is coded as a children's toy. You know, the tolerances for heavy metals in children's toys aren't—"

"It's a clear mistake. That's an erroneous result. Someone hit the wrong key and typed an incorrect number. Or perhaps someone input the tolerances for a different product. Or they miscoded the prod-uct. That happens all the time." He waved his hands in two small, loopy circles. "It could be any one of a dozen innocent explanations."

"It could be, and it probably is," she agreed. "But, as I understand the existing regulations, I need to retest the sample to confirm that."

"No, you need to focus on populating your database."

They looked at each other in silence. She could

feel her pulse throbbing in her neck. Finally, she said, "Respectfully, Mr. Jefferson, I'm not going to sign off on this batch of product without retesting."

He raised his eyebrows. "Luckily, Dr. Agarwal, you don't have to sign off on it. I will. Is that the report?"

"Yes." Her hands tightened reflexively around the papers.

"Wonderful. Thank you for hand delivering it. You may leave it on my desk."

"Mr. Jefferson—"

He drew his hand through the air in a short horizontal gesture as though he were a conductor and she were a member of his orchestra. "That'll be all. You need to get back to your project." He turned away, tapped a key to wake up his computer monitor, and started typing rapidly.

She stood there awkwardly, but he continued to pointedly ignore her. She took one last look at the report in her hand then placed it on the edge of his desk. Her legs shook as she turned and walked out of his office. As she left, she slammed the door behind her in a futile, livid gesture. She thought she heard a thud and a crash from inside the office but couldn't be sure over the angry pounding of her heart.

5

Through the living room window, Leo could see Maisy standing on the front porch, her finger hovering in the air a quarter of an inch away from the doorbell. He turned and did a quick sweep of the room. He grabbed Fiona's avocado-stained leggings and the pile of dirty miniature socks that had never quite made it into the mudroom and the washing machine and shoved them under the coffee table. Finn, engrossed in a board book that he was holding upside down, ignored the whirlwind of activity as Leo straightened piles of books, plumped up pillows, and wrangled stray blocks. Fiona abandoned her shape-sorting puzzle and toddled around the room after him, babbling.

Mocha, who evidently thought this was a game, chased her. The three of them circled the room like a tornado until Maisy finally pressed the bell.

Leo opened the door.

"Didn't you catch up with Sasha? She said she was meeting you for a drink." Maybe they'd gotten their signals crossed.

Maisy's bright eyes clouded, and she opened her mouth to answer. Before she had the chance, Fiona came careening toward the door.

"May-may!" she cooed in excitement.

Maisy was among her favorite adults in the world.

Leo ushered Maisy inside, and Fiona promptly tried to climb up her leg. Maisy reached down and scooped her up into a big hug. The action drew Finn's attention away from his book. When he spied their visitor, a huge, sleepy smile broke out over his entire face. Maisy grinned back at him.

"Hi, buddy," she sang as she carried Fiona over to her brother and placed her down beside him. She ruffled Finn's hair and gave him a smooch on the head before standing up and turning to face Leo.

"Is everything okay?" he asked.

Maisy glanced back at the twins before answering. Then she said in her reassuring, newscaster's voice, "Don't be worried, but Sasha's going to be a little late tonight."

"Why?"

"There was a little dustup at the bar."

Her failure to elaborate and the shadow of worry over her face weren't reassuring. "What kind of dustup?"

"Well, some creep was hassling this woman. He was really out of bounds."

Leo sighed. "Let me guess. Sasha decided to step in."

"Leo, this guy really was harassing her. And nobody else was doing anything, so—"

"Where is she now, Maisy?" he cut off her defense of his wife's hero complex.

Maisy took her time answering. "She's at the county jail."

He cocked his head, confused. "Why?"

"Um, she was arrested."

"They arrested her for telling off some pervert? Was she disturbing the peace?" He'd be the first to admit that his Irish-Russian wife had a temper, but she rarely even raised her voice. The quieter she got, the more trouble you were in.

"Not exactly. It got physical. Don't worry, though, she's not hurt."

Leo's stomach sank to the floor like a stone.

"How badly did she hurt the guy?" he asked.

Then he turned and noticed that the twins were watching their faces. He had no idea how much of the conversation a pair of eighteen-month olds could understand, but he was sure they could tell from the energy in the room that something was wrong. He forced himself to smile at them and raised his hand for Maisy to hold her thought.

Squatting next to them on the rug, he said. "Mama's going to be late tonight. Do you want a cookie?"

At the mention of a treat that Sasha doled out stingily, they both squealed and clapped their hands.

"Cookies? At this hour? I mean, I'm no parenting expert, but are you sure that's a good idea?" Maisy asked, wrinkling her forehead in concern.

He snorted. "Are you kidding me? They're not really cookies. They're some sort of whole-grain honey-date bar that Sasha lets them eat once in a while. They're fine. More importantly, gnawing on the bars will keep them busy while we talk."

He jogged out to the kitchen to grab two of the bars while Java wound around his ankles. He returned, handed the treats to the twins, and led Maisy to the pair of club chairs that flanked the fireplace.

"What did she do?" he asked in a low voice.

"I think she broke his nose and might've messed up his mouth a little bit. It was hard to tell with all the blood. But that's it. Oh, and she knocked the wind out of him. He did try to take a swing at her with a beer bottle, though. So I'd say he earned it."

He pinched his forehead, right above the bridge of his nose, to fend off a building tension headache. "And they took her into custody?"

"Yeah. He insisted on pressing charges. He was pretty fired up."

"I can imagine."

"Will and Naya are on their way to post her bond. I'm sure they'll get her out of there as quickly as humanly possible."

He nodded. He was sure they would, too. But still.

"Maisy, you saw it go down. Is there a chance she's in real trouble here?"

She thought it over. Then she said, "I don't

think so, sugar. There were loads of witnesses. And, you know, I'm not a potted plant. I exchanged contact information with the three women he was harassing. The police interviewed a bunch of people, too. I'm sure once that guy calms down, the whole thing will go away."

"Okay. Thanks for coming in person to let me know," he said heavily as he moved toward the door.

"Oh no you don't. I'm staying right here with you until Sasha comes home."

He considered protesting. But it would be short-sighted, to say the least, to turn down an extra set of hands at bedtime. "Thanks."

She walked over to the twins to talk to them about their cookies. He stared out the window at the night sky and tried, with limited success, not to worry about Sasha.

6

Sasha stood in the very center of the holding cell. She wished she could sit down, but she didn't trust the corroded-looking bench that ran along the wall. Her feet ached in her heels, but she had no intention of taking them off and going barefoot. Her main goal was to get out of there without having touched anything. The last thing she needed was to pick up some exotic jailhouse germ and transmit it to the twins. So she stood, upright and away from all surfaces, like a statue, and waited for Will to show up.

As the police had taken her out of the bar in handcuffs, she'd told Maisy to let Connelly know what was happening. She had to save her one phone call for her lawyer, not her husband, and besides she didn't want to be the one to break the news of her arrest to her federal agent husband. She couldn't imagine how he would respond.

She wished the booking officer hadn't taken her watch along with her phone. She had no idea what time it was or how long she'd been there. The sliver of sky she could see through the bars was purple. It was past sunset, that much she knew. Finn would be getting fussy, looking for a back rub and a lullaby. Fiona would be ramping up her nightly 'running from sleep' routine. This was the part of the evening that always went more smoothly with two parents home. A man-to-man defense was, after all, more effective than playing the zone. The threat of tears pricked her eyes so she bit down on the inside of her cheek and told herself to think about something—anything—else. Anything but her family.

Her thoughts turned to the jagoff from the bar. As far as she knew, he was still at the hospital. While they'd both been taken into custody, the police had taken the guy directly to the emergency room to have his nose and mouth checked out. She could have told them his nose was broken and he probably had a few loose teeth but had wisely kept her diagnosis to herself.

The arresting officer had been professional and—considering the circumstances—borderline kind. In the beginning, before she realized that he was actually going to take her into custody and shut her trap, she'd said she wasn't interested in pressing charges against the man, but Officer Olewine had shaken his head at her naivety and said, "Whether the charges stick or not, he probably took one look at you and smelled money—you have that well-off vibe. Plus, he just had his ass handed to him by a pocket-sized woman. His ego's not going to let you off that easy. Keep a card in your pocket, Ms. McCandless-Connelly."

It was shortly after that friendly piece of advice that she told the officer she wouldn't be answering any more questions without her lawyer present. Which reminded her, where in the world was he? Patience wasn't her strong suit under the best of circumstances. And nobody would mistake standing in a filthy jail cell as the best of circumstances.

Maybe some mindful breathing would help.

She closed her eyes and connected with her breath.

Inhale. Sloooow exhale. Inhale.

She opened her eyes and wondered how much time had passed now. Probably fifteen seconds, she told herself. She wished she had something to read —a book, a magazine, the back of a cereal box.

She shut her eyes. *Inhale. Slooooooooower exhale. Inhale.*

Footsteps rang out in the hallway. Her eyes popped open.

"Well, counselor, she's all yours," said a corrections officer she hadn't seen before as he unlocked the barred door.

Will, looking as fresh and impeccable as he'd been when she last saw him at the office, shook his head at her. "A bar fight? Really."

She shot him a dark look that said *"Can we talk about this later?"*

"Let's go sign out your personal items. At least you got to keep your clothes. The booking officer tells me they don't have any jumpsuits small enough for you and the juvenile facility didn't answer when they called over for a loaner."

He led her through the process of reclaiming her phone, watch, and handbag. Then he put a hand on the small of her back and piloted her away from the lobby doors.

"What are you doing? The exit's that way."

He stopped walking and looked down at her. "You're something of a minor celebrity to begin with, given your colorful history. When the news broke that you were arrested for beating up a man in a bar, KDKA, WPXI, and WTAE probably got in a street race to be the first camera crew here. I wouldn't be surprised if there are print journalists camped out there, too."

Her stomach lurched toward her knees. "I can't—"

"You're not going to. This isn't my first rodeo, you know."

He pushed open a metal door and started down the stairwell. She followed, shaken by the thought of being ambushed by the press. When they reached the basement, he turned down a short hallway and nodded to a jail guard standing by a large roll-up delivery door.

The officer nodded back to Will. Then he hit a button and the door lifted.

"Is he on the take?" she whispered loudly as they walked out onto a loading dock.

"For heaven's sake, keep your voice down. No

he's not on the take. His son Riley played lacrosse with my youngest. He's doing us a courtesy."

"Oh. Sorry." She felt sufficiently guilty for assuming the worst.

Will's ancient Volvo station wagon was idling in the bay. Naya sat behind the wheel. Even though —or maybe because—Naya was one of her closest friends, Sasha's cheeks burned with shame. She couldn't believe her coworkers and friends were seeing her this way. Naya popped the door locks and Will hustled Sasha into the back seat.

"You should duck down. The reporters might recognize my car," he told her as he slid into the passenger seat and fastened his seat belt.

She rolled herself into the footwell. Will said to Naya, "Floor it."

The car bucked forward, and Naya careened out of the lot. Sasha considered pointing out that perhaps speeding through the county jail's parking lot wasn't the wisest decision. But since she was the only person in the car who'd been fingerprinted and had her mug shot taken that night, perhaps her advice was less valuable than she thought. She kept her thoughts to herself.

As Naya shot through the Armstrong Tunnel

and headed uptown toward Bigelow Boulevard, she called back, "It's all clear. You can sit up now."

Sasha pushed herself up from the floor and arranged herself in the backseat. Will twisted around to look at her. "Now do you want to tell us what happened?"

"There's not much to tell. I met Maisy for a drink after I filed the position statement in the arbitration. Some jerk was harassing a woman and it got out of hand," she said tiredly.

"So you broke his face?" Naya supplied helpfully.

"No. So, I walked over and told him to leave her alone. Maisy got her and her two friends away from him before he got belligerent. But he pushed me—"

"He pushed you. You're sure?" Will interjected.

She thought. "Well, he *tried* to push me," she clarified. "I grabbed his wrist and twisted him into an armlock."

Naya snorted. "As one does."

"Then what happened?" Will prompted.

"I warned him. I told him that I could break his wrist, no sweat, if I wanted to. But instead I wanted him to leave. He started gathering up his stuff, and

I guess I let my guard down. I turned my back on him and he picked up his beer bottle to take a swing at me."

"Okay, this guy sounds stupid," Naya observed.

Sasha smiled weakly. "I know, right?"

"So he hit you with the bottle and then what?"

"Hang on. He didn't hit me. There's a long mirror that runs along the wall across from the bar, and I saw him raising the bottle, so I turned around and hit him with a palm strike to the nose."

Naya fist pumped but Will fixed her with a serious look. Then he said, "And after the palm strike—which broke his nose, by the way—you punched him in the mouth and then the solar plexus?"

"More or less. I actually punched him right above his mouth—in his philtrum. After I winded him, the bouncers finally woke up and stepped in."

Will was silent. Naya turned onto Baum Boulevard, swinging out to avoid a trio of college students who were inexplicably walking in the road.

Finally, Will said, "So he didn't actually lay a hand on you. Is that right?"

"I guess that's right." She shifted in her seat.

"He was a big guy, Will. And he definitely tried to hurt me. Is it my fault I successfully protected myself?"

Naya shifted into associate mode. "Of course not. It was self-defense. You were in imminent peril."

"Was she, Naya?" Will asked in his professorial voice. "Did she really have a well-founded fear that he was going to hurt her?"

"Yes," Sasha piped up in a small voice.

"Did you? You're highly trained in hand-to-hand combat. Do you think he was?"

"Evidently not," Naya cracked.

Will shut her down with a stern look. "Listen, that's the case I made to ADA Lewis, the assistant district attorney who signed off on your arrest. And your small stature and the fact that you're a woman and a member of the bar will only help your cause, but this isn't a joke, Sasha."

She stared at him. "They're not actually going to charge me, are they? You know, I *could* have elbowed him in the throat, crushed his windpipe —if I'd wanted to."

"I don't know. I'm meeting Lewis for coffee in the morning. I'll see how persuadable he is. But let's not mention the whole crushing the windpipe thing again, shall we? Also, the three of us need to talk about whether it's a good idea for me to represent you."

"What?" She blinked.

"I'm your legal partner. Your arrest, and eventual criminal case if there is one, could impact the firm and its employees, including Naya, Caroline, and the others. It could get complicated."

"It's not complicated," Naya argued right away. "Some jagoff was pawing at some young, drunk girl, and Sasha stepped in to do the right thing. Just like you or I would have."

"Except, unlike you or I—or most people— Sasha has actually killed a man with her bare hands before."

Nino Carlucci. The rogue FBI agent who had tracked her from Pittsburgh to the Outer Banks to murder her.

"Technically, he broke his neck in a fall," she offered.

"Regardless. We're not going to turn our backs on our co-worker and friend," Naya insisted.

"And I'm not suggesting we should. I'm simply saying that the situation's still developing, and we need to make sure we support Sasha in a way that doesn't imperil the firm. That's all. With any luck, Lewis will decline to pursue the matter."

"With any luck," Naya echoed.

Sasha sat silently in the back seat. The problem with relying on luck was she only had one kind of luck---the bad kind.

7

Prachi was poring over the test results with her morning cup of tea at her elbow when a shadow fell over her desk. She looked up and blinked in surprise to see one of the building security guards looming over her.

"May I help you?"

He gave her a stern look. "Dr. Agarwal, I need you to come with me."

A dozen thoughts whirled through Prachi's brain. Someone had noticed the makeshift lab she'd surreptitiously begun to construct the night before in an unused supply room. She was no stranger to necessity and had done more with fewer resources back home in Bangalore before she'd entered the university and had gained access to its world-class laboratories. While any tests she eventually performed would fall short of the customary standards, they'd be better than nothing. And she'd be damned if she would let a product go to market when she had doubts about its safety—whether Peter Jefferson liked it or not. But who could have seen her? She'd been so careful.

"Where are we going? I have quite a lot of work to do," she finally said, trying to feign a lack of concern.

"Human resources." His voice was curt and his expression stone-faced.

Someone had definitely found out about her secret lab. Her pulse pounded as she gathered up her bag, looped the lariat with her building identification card around her neck, and powered off her computer.

The security guard led her wordlessly through the maze of cubicles to the elevator. He pressed the call button and they waited in silence for the elevator doors to open. She peeked at his ID card and noted his first name: Phil.

They entered the elevator car and stood side by side. Prachi shifted anxiously from foot to foot. She hadn't yet picked up the ability to engage in the small talk about sports and television that her coworkers seemed to enjoy. But she worried that this Phil person would misinterpret her failure to do so as a sign of guilt or malfeasance. She racked her brain, searching for a popular culture reference she could make, but finally settled for smiling weakly. He looked back at her impassively until they reached the sixth floor and the doors opened.

He gestured for her to exit first. She did. Then she dutifully waited for him to lead the way to the human resources department. He passed by the director's office and stopped in front of Maureen Glassman's door. Maureen was the senior employee responsible for hiring and retaining the company's many international workers. Phil rapped on the frosted glass door with his fist but didn't wait to be invited inside. Instead, he pushed it open and announced, "I have Dr. Agarwal, ma'am."

"Come on in, Prachi," Maureen called.

Prachi steeled herself before she crossed the threshold and entered the room. Phil positioned himself in the open doorway with his arms folded across his chest. Maureen gave him a startled look. "That'll be all, Phil."

"No, ma'am. Given the situation, I was

instructed to stay while you meet with her." His voice was firm.

The situation? Okay, they definitely knew about the lab. Prachi started formulating her defense: She hadn't taken any office supplies. She'd used her own funds to acquire the material. She hadn't even 'borrowed' a sample from the affected batch, yet. And she'd done all the work on her own time. While she was sure they would have preferred that she put in extra hours working on the database, her understanding of American labor law was that she could do as she wished outside of her scheduled work hours. She swallowed the cascade of arguments that wanted to pour forward. Better to wait to learn how much Maureen knew. There was no reason to confess to more than was necessary.

Maureen was still focused on the security guard. She said, "I appreciate management's concern, Phil. However, I know Dr. Agarwal quite well, and I'm not afraid of her."

"Sorry, ma'am." Phil gave a not-at-all-sorry shrug.

She fixed him with a sour look. "I need to speak to her in private. If you feel you must stay, you can post up outside the door."

He scratched at his crew cut while he considered the compromise. Finally, he nodded. "Okay. I guess that works." He took a step backward, turned, and closed the door behind him.

Prachi could see him through the frosted glass. He stood, blocking the doorway, with his arms folded across his chest.

She faced Maureen. Because she couldn't imagine what to say, she said nothing at all.

Maureen took a lined notepad and pen from a pile behind her and placed them precisely in the center of her desk. After they were arranged to her liking, she said, "Please have a seat, Dr. Agarwal."

Prachi scurried to the visitor's chair and sat the way she'd been taught at grammar school: knees together; ankles crossed; her hands primly interlaced in her lap.

"I imagine you know why you're here," Maureen began.

"Actually, I'm not entirely sure."

She gave Prachi a close look.

"You're fortunate that Mr. Jefferson chose not press charges against you. But this is still a serious situation."

Charges? Prachi squinted at her. "I'm afraid I don't understand."

"It's very simple. Your behavior in his office—throwing a picture frame at him and breaking the glass—technically qualifies as an assault. He would be well within his right to call the police. But as it is, he's not even making a formal workplace complaint provided you attend an anger management class and there are no further infractions."

Prachi stared at her wordlessly.

She went on. "Frankly, I think the only reason he's being so gracious is that we're backed into a corner on this database project. We can't very well revoke our sponsorship of your visa and send you home."

"I didn't throw anything at Mr. Jefferson," she finally managed to say. "I have no idea what you're talking about."

"I saw the broken glass in his office. He said you flew into a rage when he told you there's no room in the budget for an assistant to help you with data entry."

"I didn't—"

"I do understand that you're under a lot of pressure, Prachi, and that the timeline is tight. But's it just not professional to have an outburst like that. At least, it's not in keeping with our workplace culture."

"That's not what happened," Prachi protested.

The sympathy drained from Maureen's face and she held up a hand. "Please stop. I'm not debating this with you. If you're going to continue to work here, you're required to take an anger management class."

Prachi bit down hard on her lower lip. This was not the time to say what she was thinking. "I understand."

"Good. Now, if there's nothing else we need to discuss, I'll—"

"Actually, there is." Despite her best efforts, Prachi simply couldn't stop herself. "You should know that Peter Jefferson is going to sell a product that hasn't passed the requisite heavy metals testing."

Maureen's voice was like ice water. "Don't even bother. He predicted you'd try to concoct a counter-story. Until you've completed the anger management course, you are not to have any direct contact with Peter. You'll need to go through my office if you need to interact with anyone in Product Development and Innovation. Are we clear?"

"Yes. Crystal." She dug her fingernails into her

palms. She had to get out of this office before she really did lose her temper.

And then the memory of slamming Mr. Jefferson's office door flashed through her mind. The force must've knocked over a picture frame on his desk and broken it. But why on earth would he tell Maureen she'd thrown it at him? It made no sense —no, actually, it made all the sense in the world. By claiming she'd gotten violent, he'd effectively forestalled her from making a stink about the testing results or, at a minimum, guaranteed that no one would believe her if she did.

Maureen was watching her face, so Prachi attempted a smile. "I apologize for letting my temper get the best of me. May I go now? I do have quite a lot of work to do."

"Of course. Here's the information about the anger management program. This particular class is for women only. I think it could help you a good bit." She extended an envelope toward Prachi.

Prachi hesitated—her fingers hovering inches from the paper—then, as resignation settled in her gut, she plucked it from between Maureen's fingers. "Thanks," she mumbled.

"I hope you know I don't want you to fail—I want you to succeed."

She couldn't bring herself to respond to Maureen's treacly tone. She bobbed her head.

"That'll be all. Phil will walk you back to your work station."

8

An unfamiliar wave of self-consciousness hit Sasha as she walked into the Law Offices of McCandless & Volmer. She told herself she was being silly. The people who worked with her and Will weren't just employees or colleagues—they were among her closest friends. Nobody in the firm was going to judge her. She'd been dreading this moment since Will and Naya had picked her up from jail the night before.

Even when they dropped her off—in the sanctuary of her own home—she could barely meet Connelly's eyes. Thanks to Maisy's help, he'd put the twins to bed, and they were sleeping soundly.

Sasha had stood in the nursery for a long time, looking down at them as if she were trying to memorize every small detail—Finn's cherub cheeks, rosy and fat; the way Fiona threw her arm over her brother, protective of him even in sleep. Connelly had crept into the room and stood beside her. He'd wrapped his arm around her waist and murmured in her ear that everything was going to be okay.

She'd slept fitfully and woke with a knot in the pit of her stomach at the thought of going to work. It was a sensation she hadn't felt since her associate days at Prescott & Talbott. But she wasn't an associate; she was a name partner and a principal in the firm, which meant she needed to get her butt into the office and run her business. So she'd showered, gulped down her morning coffee, and snuck out of the house while Leo and the kids were still sleeping.

Now she hesitated outside the lobby door. *You didn't do anything wrong*, she reminded herself. As far as mantras went, it had limited effectiveness. But it gave her the determination she needed to push the door open and hurry through the lobby. She breezed by the reception desk with her head down and mumbled a hello in the general direction of Kim, the friendliest of their receptionists—the one who always asked after the twins.

Once she was safely ensconced in her office, she closed the door firmly behind her and leaned against it for a moment. A knock sounded from the other side, startling her.

"Mac?" Naya's voice called. "Open up. I have coffee."

She turned and opened the door. Naya extended an oversized mug from Jake's.

She took it gratefully. "Thanks."

Naya narrowed her eyes. "I figured you could use a boost. And I know you don't need a lecture."

"But?" Sasha sipped the coffee and waited for whatever scolding was coming.

"But you can't hide in here forever. It makes you look guilty."

"I'm embarrassed."

"So? Get over it. Do you think you were wrong to help that drunk girl?"

"No. But ..."

"But what? But nothing. If you think you did the right thing, act like it already."

She would have answered, but Naya was

already walking away. She left her door ajar and took her coffee to her desk and powered up her laptop.

Naya's words rattled around in her brain while she went through her morning routine of answering emails and reading legal articles online.

She had just pulled up a set of interrogatories that she needed to answer when someone rapped on her office door. The door swung in, and Jordana, the part-time filing clerk, stuck her head in.

"Hey, Sasha."

"Why aren't you in school?"

Jordana was still in high school, so she mainly worked summers, school holidays, and a few weekend hours, here and there.

"Administrative day. My mom didn't want me to spend the day at home playing Minecraft, so I asked Naya to schedule me."

"Are you doing anything interesting?" Sasha asked, already knowing what the answer would be. To Jordana, it was all interesting—even the most mundane work seemed glamorous to the teen.

"Yes! I'm helping Caroline organize all the articles that Will's written. He's published a lot. I'm reading them as we go. He's been involved in some cool criminal cases."

Sasha couldn't help but smile at the girl's enthusiasm. Will had definitely handled some interesting representations in the course of his white-collar defense career. But she'd read enough of his writing to know that 'dry' was the most apt descriptor.

"Great. So what can I do for you?"

"Will asked Caroline if you were in yet, so I said I'd walk down and check. He wants you to stop by when it's convenient."

"Tell him I'll come to see him after I answer these interrogatories."

"Will do." Jordana nodded before disappearing from view.

The interrogatories weren't all that pressing, but she knew that Will would likely want to discuss his breakfast meeting with the district attorney's office, which would no doubt prove distracting. And she needed to focus on work for at least part of the day.

WILL'S DOOR WAS OPEN, so she walked in.

"I heard you wanted to see me."

He looked up from The Wall Street Journal. "Did you get your interrogatories taken care of?"

"Pretty much."

"Good. And how are you feeling this morning?"

"Fine."

He studied her face. "Are you sure?"

"Positive. To be completely honest, I was feeling ashamed of myself, but I had a conversation that reminded me I didn't do anything wrong." She gave him a level look. "If I could go back in time, I don't think I'd do anything differently."

He frowned. "In that case, I admire your conviction, but I'm afraid you aren't going to like what I have to report. Pull up a seat."

She took the visitor's chair across from him and braced for the worst. "You met with ADA Lewis?"

"I did. The man you beat up is a fellow by the name of Steve Harold. There's no dispute about the fact that Mr. Harold was pestering those three young women. Lewis said that the witness statements from all support your version of events. And Annie, the woman who was the target of Mr. Harold's attention, told the interviewer that she and her friends were beginning to feel very unsafe and were unsure about what to do when you came over."

So far, this didn't sound bad, but Will's serious expression kept her from getting her hopes up.

He continued. "While it's lucky for them that you were there, it's perhaps unlucky for you."

"Didn't the witnesses corroborate that Harold took the first swing? He tried to lay hands on me first."

Will nodded. "Yes, Lewis agrees that it went down that way."

"So what's the problem? I was in imminent peril of bodily harm." She was rusty on her criminal self-defense theories, but even a first-year law student knew imminent peril.

"Ah, but there's the rub. The district attorney isn't so sure you were. Mr. Lewis noted that you're highly trained in self-defense and hand-to-hand combat. So you were far more equipped than the ordinary person to handle yourself in a physical altercation. And the hapless Mr. Harold never actually laid hands on you, did he? He tried to push you and you neutralized him. Then he attempted to hit you with a bottle, and you, well, you incapacitated him."

"Are you saying I should have let him push me —or crack me over the head with a bottle?" Surely that's not what he was saying.

"I know it sounds ludicrous, but that is Lewis's position. He believes you may have responded with greater force than was commensurate to the threat you faced." Will delivered the news in a sad tone.

"How can he mean that? I mean, look at me." All her life, she'd been underestimated because of her size. Now, finally, someone was going to discount the fact that she was not quite five feet tall and just shy of a hundred pounds, and it was going to inure to her detriment? What a crock.

Will nodded and his voice took on the faintest hint of hope. "Right. Lewis knows if this goes to a jury they're going to take one look at you—especially compared to Mr. Harold—and return a swift not guilty verdict."

"So .... What's the problem?"

"The problem is that Harold's causing a real

ruckus. But I think I've worked out a deal with the district attorney's office."

A deal. She didn't like the sound of a deal. "You know I'm not going to admit to any wrongdoing, right? Because I didn't do anything wrong."

"I surmised as much." He stood and walked around to the front of his desk. He leaned against it and looked down at her. "You and I and the district attorney's office all know that their case is a loser. But we all also know that the process of going to trial will harm your reputation and possibly the firm's, as well. You need to think about your employees and your family."

"But—"

"If you thought it was embarrassing to be fingerprinted and photographed for a mug shot, you really won't enjoy being dragged through the mud in a criminal trial."

"I know that, Will."

He kept talking. "Everything will be fair game, and—"

It was her turn to interrupt. "What do you mean, *everything*? I don't have anything to hide," she bristled.

"Come on, Sasha. Be realistic. You've been

involved in how many situations where the police were called?" He started ticking off names on his fingers. "Laura Peterson; those sisters up in Firetown; Jeffrey Bricker; the knife fight with the coroner—"

That was a bridge too far. "Hang on, wait a minute. It wasn't a knife fight. It was a stabbing—and I was the victim."

"And, then, of course, there's the FBI agent whose neck you broke—and that's just a partial list."

"He fell," she argued, frustrated and flustered.

"You see? They'll bring up each of your past ... escapades, and you'll be forced to explain. And you know what Noah always used to say."

"If you're explaining, you're losing."

"Precisely. Now, again, I don't think you'd lose in the sense of a guilty verdict. But I'm confident reliving each of those events in public would be difficult, demoralizing, and damaging."

"How would that all even be admissible? It's past conduct." She hated the panic she heard in her voice.

"Perhaps. Or it perhaps would be deemed admissible to show pattern and practice. Do you really want to find out? Or do you want to agree to

Accelerated Rehabilitative Disposition without entering a guilty plea?"

She narrowed her eyes. "That's the deal? ARD?"

"Yes. You'd be on probation for six months and you would have to complete a court-supervised anger management program for first-time female offenders."

She shook her head. "Will, I really don't think that's called for."

"Your record would be expunged. You wouldn't have to report anything to the Bar."

She stared at him wordlessly.

"Honestly," he continued, "it's probably no more painful than the average CLE course."

"Did you really just equate a court-supervised anger management program for criminal offenders with a continuing legal education class?" He was pulling out all the stops.

"It's a fair offer—it's more than fair. It's a get out of jail free card. At least talk it over with Leo."

She stood, her pulse thumping in her throat. "I will. And listen, it's not that I'm not grateful for what you've done, meeting with Lewis and getting him to make the deal. It's just ..."

He studied her face for a moment after she

trailed off. "It's just that you don't believe you did anything wrong. I know. But I also know that clients tend to get nervous when their lawyers are caught up in criminal investigations."

Something in the way he said it gave her pause. "Did a specific client say something already?"

He pulled the day's *Pittsburgh Legal Journal* out from underneath *The Wall Street Journal* that he'd been reading and handed it to her. "Not yet. But you made the PLJ."

She skimmed the article—more of an item, really. There was no accompanying photograph (thank goodness) and the tidbit took up less than an inch of print:

McCandless & Volmer partner Sasha McCandless-Connelly was arrested last night after a brawl erupted at a popular Downtown bar. No details were available. Central processing officials at the Allegheny County Jail did not return our call. McCandless-Connelly, formerly of Prescott & Talbott, is no stranger to these pages, having been involved in several high-profile criminal matters over the years. McCandless & Volmer partner Will Volmer, who is believed to be representing McCandless-Connelly, declined to comment citing a pending investigation.

She looked up. "No comment?"

"We need to craft a cogent media strategy, Sasha. And a message for our clients—and our employees."

Will looked tired, like he was carrying a heavy burden, which, of course, he was. And knowing that she was the yoke on his back filled her with guilt.

"Okay. I'll talk to Connelly today and let you know about the deal." She handed the newspaper back to him.

"That would be a good first step."

SASHA SLID into the booth beside Connelly and leaned in for a kiss.

"Thanks for meeting me."

"A late breakfast with my lovely wife—who would say no to that? Your mom was thrilled to have a couple hours with the kids. Coffee's on its way."

She smiled. Breakfast at Pamela's had been a tradition since before they were married. In fact, they'd shared their first table at Pamela's back when Connelly was just the irritating federal agent who wouldn't leave her alone for her own safety. Now he was her rock, her world.

She angled herself in the booth and took his large hands in hers. "So, this isn't just an impromptu date. There's something I want to talk about."

Connelly flashed a crooked grin. "I know. Will called me."

A frisson of surprise and irritation zipped through her. "Will shared our conversation with you? That's supposed to be privileged."

He shot her an 'oh, come on' look. "He didn't divulge the substance of your conversation. He told me that the two of you talked about a deal the district attorney's office was offering."

"That's all he said?" She narrowed her eyes.

"He also said that he'd encouraged you to talk it over with me. He said he was giving me a head's up because it would be good if we could arrange a time to discuss it without Finn and Fiona doing their monkey imitations in the background."

It all sounded eminently reasonable. And yet the suspicion that she was being managed lingered. She might have pressed the issue, but Becca, their favorite waitress, appeared with a carafe of coffee.

"I'm just gonna leave this here for you two because I can't be running back and forth all morning," she cracked.

"Thanks, Becca."

"The usual—a tall stack with a side of bacon and an omelet with dry wheat toast?" she asked, her pencil poised.

"Yep." Pamela's might be famous for its pancakes—and Connelly certainly loved them; but Sasha was in it for the eggs.

Becca headed off to put in their order, and Connelly locked eyes with Sasha.

"Tell me about the deal."

Sasha's anger clashed into her worry; together, they threatened to pour out. She inhaled then exhaled slowly before answering. "The district attorney wants me to agree to ARD."

"English, please."

"Alternative Rehabilitative Disposition—it's a program for first-time offenders. If I were to go through the program, I wouldn't have to go to trial."

"Would you have to plead to anything?"

"Well, no. But I'd have to go through an anger management program, Connelly."

He cocked his head. "But no guilty plea?"

"Right. But do you really think a jury would find me guilty, anyway?"

"I don't know the details, but from what little you told me last night, of course not." His gray eyes were thoughtful. "But Will is usually pretty sensible. So why does he think you should take the deal?"

She tapped her fingernails on the side of her porcelain mug as she answered. "He thinks that even though I'd ultimately win at trial, the publicity would be bad for us—our family and the firm. So, basically to avoid a smear campaign, I'm supposed to bow to this demand even though I didn't do anything wrong."

He didn't answer right away. "But you don't have to admit that you did anything wrong."

"Sure, I don't have to enter a guilty plea, but, come on, we both know how taking a deal looks."

He shrugged. "I guess you could view at it as conceding something. Or you could just look at it as being conservative in an attempt to protect people you care about."

Her chest tightened, and she pushed her mug away. "So you're saying I should take the deal?"

"Nope. That's not my decision to make. *You*

have to decide. I'm just saying there are two ways to look at it." His voice was low and gentle.

"Do you think I need to take an anger management class?"

"Far be it from me to tell the woman who broke my nose and stole my gun the first time I met her that she has a quick temper," he teased.

She laughed despite herself. "Noted. Listen, I appreciate that you respect my right to make up my own mind. But we *are* a team. I'd like to know what you think of the deal."

"I guess I'm not quite as brave as you are. I don't want to see my wife risk jail time, the loss of her legal license, and her standing in the community just to prove a point. If you know you didn't do anything wrong, that's all that matters."

She stared at her husband for a long moment, taking in the contours of his face, the shape of his eyes, his lopsided smile. Finally, she said aloud what she had not yet admitted to herself, "I'm scared. Really scared. I haven't felt this way since right after Wally stabbed me."

Just then, Becca returned with their plates. She must have sensed the mood at the table because she dropped off their food and left without making any conversation. Sasha looked down at her eggs and wondered if she'd be able to force herself to eat them.

Connelly didn't touch his fork. Instead, he took her face in his hands. "You don't spook easily. What's going on?"

"I just have this feeling—" she trailed off and shivered. "The whole thing feels wrong to me, like a trap."

"Do you mean the ARD offer?" he probed.

"All of it. This is like one of those kids' choose your own adventure books—only with no good choices. No matter which path I pick, I have a hunch it's going to be a bad one."

He poured a small lake of syrup over his hot cakes and said, "Which feels like the least bad choice?"

She shook her head in frustration. "I don't know. I think taking the deal and agreeing to ARD is less risky."

"The worst possible outcome if you roll the dice and go to trial is pretty bad—jail time, right?"

"Right."

"What's the worst possible outcome if you take the deal?"

Her eyes filled with tears. "I won't be able to live with myself for being a coward."

"Seems like you might want to reexamine how you define bravery."

She blinked back the tears and looked at him through her now-wet eyelashes. "I guess so."

He reached over and tucked a loose strand of hair behind her ear. "Your omelet's getting cold."

9

Prachi glanced down the corridor one way and then the other to confirm that nobody was coming. She hadn't planned to take the samples this soon, but she'd found the storage room on a building map. When she'd walked by to scout it out, two facts had jumped out at her: one, despite its label on the map it was large, much larger than its description as a 'closet' suggested; and, two, to her amazement, it wasn't locked.

She'd decided then and there to take the products she needed before someone realized their error—if it was an error—and locked the door. She wasn't yet ready to test the samples, but she'd find a place to keep them hidden until the time came. First things first, she told herself. Get them now.

She was jumpy and ill-prepared but determined not to let this opportunity slip out of her grasp. She furtively pushed open the storeroom door and slipped inside. She didn't know where the wall lights were located, but she had a small flashlight attached to the strap of her purse—a holdover from the year her student housing had come complete with spotty electricity. She clicked it on and scanned the room for the light switch.

As she reached up to flip the switch her heart caught in her throat. What if someone saw a square of light spilling out from under the door and came to investigate?

She pulled her hand back from the switch plate as if it were a hot stove and aimed her puny flashlight beam at the crooked rows of pallets, piled high with boxes. Given the disorganized nature of the company, she imagined it would be too much to hope that they were in any kind of order. She read off the printed labels as she picked through the rows:

AL180; AP022. Good. Alphabetical order would be perfect.

Then the system broke down. *JM773; PP119; LI441.* She muttered under her breath.

She finally located the cluster of pallets holding AR462 sandwiched between NE004 and DL215. Her hands shook as she used the letter opener from her desk to cut a slit in the packing tape. She eased three packages through the opening and then resealed it as best she could. She grimaced at the realization that she hadn't thought to bring a bag or tote to transport the products to her laboratory. She swung the flashlight around the storage room in a weak arc of light but saw no trash bags or buckets or anything that would be useful for concealing the packages. She shrugged out of her white lab coat—it was a hilarious costume anyway, considering that she functioned as a glorified data entry clerk. She wrapped the coat around the three shrink-wrapped, cardboard-backed retail sets and draped the long end of the coat over her arm.

She filled her lungs with air, pulled the windowless metal door open, and strode out into the empty hallway as casually as she could. She forced herself to walk until she reached the end of the corridor. Then she turned right and broke into a jog as she made her way to the staircase that led to her office three floors up, her heart pounding in her ears and her breath coming shallow and fast. *She'd done it.*

10

S asha shifted in the metal chair, trying and failing to achieve a comfortable position, and looked around. There were a dozen of the chairs with attached half-desks arranged in a circle but only five—including hers—were occupied. Her four fellow anger management students wore expressions ranging from bored to scared to, well, angry.

No one seemed particularly happy to be there, but who would be? The best thing Sasha could say for the program so far was that the class was held in a community-based probation office that was within walking distance of both her office and her home and was conveniently scheduled for six o'clock in the evening. She could even swing by the market on her way home and pick up some apples. Satisfied with her efforts to find something positive in her current situation, she settled back and waited.

The room was painted an institutional green-gray. The two windows were small and high on the walls—too high for daydreamers to gaze out. A plain-looking clock and a whiteboard hung on the front wall. She ranked the ambiance somewhere above the holding cell but below her mechanic's waiting room.

After several minutes, the uncomfortable silence that blanketed the room was broken by the squeak of the under-oiled metal door to the class-room swinging open. A gray-haired woman walked in and scanned the room.

"I'm Karen Hogan. You may call me Mrs. Hogan. I'm a social worker and I'll be facilitating this group. Today we're going to start by setting out the ground rules and my expectations for you and talk about what we hope to achieve during our eight weeks together," she said crisply.

She had the air of a no-nonsense teacher who would impose strict order on a classroom full of unruly middle schoolers. Despite the fact that she was decades removed from junior high, Sasha sat up a little straighter and fixed her eyes on the woman.

Karen Hogan picked up a dry erase marker and wrote her name on the white board at the front of the room: *Mrs. Hogan.* Then she recapped the marker, turned, and held up the fingers of her right hand as she ticked off the rules. "One, the most important rule is that you must attend each session and work honestly and sincerely on your anger problem. I will not sign off that you've completed the course unless you put in the time and do the work. There are eight classes, and I expect you to attend eight classes—arriving on time, ready to address your issues."

The bored teenager raised her hand. "What if we get sick?"

"Unless you're in the hospital, you need to come to class. If you *do* have the misfortune to be hospitalized, you should hope it's a quick stay. If you miss two classes, you're done."

"Done?" the teenage girl echoed.

"As in removed from the program. This is serious business, ladies. You're here because you need help. I can only help you if you show up."

Sasha felt herself bristling. The Indian woman sitting two seats away frowned.

"Are we all perfectly clear on the attendance policy?" Mrs. Hogan asked.

A series of halfhearted "yeses" rose from the circle. Sasha couldn't bring herself to join the singsong chorus, so she nodded.

"Good. Rule number two, you have to be truthful and real; otherwise, you aren't going to get anything out of this. Finally, three, we work for fifty minutes. We will have one ten-minute break at the twenty-five minute mark. Don't come back late. The door will be locked." She paused to let the information sink in.

She's trying to get a rise out of us, Sasha told herself. *Don't take the bait.*

The women stared back at Mrs. Hogan silently.

"Now that we've got that out of the way, let's go around the circle. Introduce yourself and explain what brought you here. We'll start with you." She nodded at the girl who asked the question about absences.

"I'm Lani. And, um, I'm here because I got into an argument with my foster mom and pushed her."

"And what was the argument about, Lani?" Mrs. Hogan asked in a tone that left no doubt she already knew the answer.

"Curfew."

Apparently Lani was a woman of few words. She settled back into her chair and gave Mrs. Hogan a blank look.

The sour-looking woman sitting next to Lani spoke up. "My name is Carla Fisher. My ex-husband and I were fighting about the visitation schedule. He brought the kids back two hours late."

"So what did you do?"

Carla lowered her eyes. "Slashed the dirtbag's tires."

"I see," Mrs. Hogan murmured.

Sasha was next. She considered how much she wanted to share with the group. The actual answer, of course, was not a blessed thing, but she had to say something. "I'm Sasha McCandless-Connelly. I'm here because I was involved in an altercation at a bar."

Karen Hogan's face registered no emotion but Lani leaned across Carla and said, "*You* were in a bar fight? With who—a Keebler elf?" The crack earned a snort from Carla and a reproving shake of the head from Mrs. Hogan.

"Actually, I was in a bar fight with a man who was harassing a woman. I stepped in and stopped him." She regretted the words as soon as they flew out of her mouth.

"It sounds to me like you're still defending your behavior."

Sasha clenched her teeth and nodded.

"Don't worry; we'll be working on owning our actions," Mrs. Hogan assured her.

Next was Gracelyn, who explained that she worked as a flagger for a road crew. "So I was holding a stop sign, and this jagoff drove his BMW right through the work area without obeying the sign."

"Mmm-hmm," Mrs. Hogan prompted.

"So I reached through his open window and grabbed him by the shirt."

"And you do understand that was not an appropriate response, correct?"

"Yeah," Gracelyn mumbled.

Everyone turned to the last woman. "My name is Prachi Agarwal. I am here for no reason."

One silver eyebrow shot up. Then Mrs. Hogan said, "Are you trying to tell us you don't know why you're here, Ms. Agarwal?"

"It's Dr. Agarwal, actually. And no, I know why I'm here. I have to attend this class as a condition of my continued employment. Otherwise my visa will be revoked, and I'll have to leave the country. But I didn't do anything."

"Another defensive posture," Mrs. Hogan observed.

"No, I'm not defending something I did. I literally didn't do anything. I'm being railroaded because I brought a problem to the attention of management—"

Mrs. Hogan's hand shot up. "Let me stop you right there, Prachi. Rule number two is to be honest." She looked down at her clipboard. "You threw a picture frame at an executive vice president. You simply cannot assault your coworkers."

"I didn't."

"You're not going to get anything from this class unless you are open and truthful about your problem." Mrs. Hogan's voice was icy.

Prachi muttered something under her breath, which Mrs. Hogan must have heard but chose to disregard. Instead, she walked around the circle handing out notebooks and pens along with copies of a syllabus and a handout that listed the physiological signs of rising anger. Then she set a timer for ten minutes and told them their first exercise was to write a list of all the tools they currently used to manage their anger.

Sasha started out with the old standbys—taking a deep breath; counting to ten; walking around the block—then moved on to the mindfulness and meditation techniques she'd been working on. As she reached the end of the page, she glanced up to see if everyone else was still writing. Three other pens were still moving. Prachi Agarwal stared stone-faced at a blank sheet of paper, her pen capped and on the desk in front of her.

THE METAL DOOR to the snack room swung open. Prachi wiped away her tears, mortified that someone was going to see her crying. She'd assumed all her classmates had gone out to smoke cigarettes during their ten-minute respite, but the door opened to reveal the miniature brunette bar fighter standing in the doorway.

She regarded Prachi with an expression of warm concern, which had the unfortunate effect of making Prachi cry harder. Prachi buried her face in her hands.

"Hey, hey," the woman—Sasha with the hyphenated name—said as she walked quickly across the linoleum floor. "Are you okay?" she crouched beside Prachi's chair.

Prachi peeked out at her from between her hands. "No, I suppose I'm not okay." She spoke haltingly as she tried to explain, "I don't belong here. I don't have an anger problem."

The other woman chose her words with care. "Regardless of whether you think you should be here, it's clear that Karen Hogan's not going to let any of us get out of saying that we have a problem. My unsolicited, free advice, which is worth exactly what you pay for it, is to get with the program. Do the exercises and tell her what she wants to hear, so you can get on with your life."

Prachi stared at her in amazement. Were all Americans so pragmatic and unprincipled?

"Why should I say I have a problem that I don't have?" Her frustration rose, and she slammed her hands down on the table in front of her.

Sasha raised an eyebrow and said pointedly, "I'm pretty sure that's the sort of thing Karen doesn't want us to be doing."

Prachi laughed weakly. "Okay, I freely admit that I'm frustrated. But that's because I've been sent to this class to solve a problem I don't have. It's absurd."

Sasha nodded and glanced behind her as if she wanted to confirm nobody could hear her. "Just between me and you and the vending machine, I couldn't agree more. I stopped a man from sexually assaulting a young woman who'd had too much to drink. For my troubles, he tried to attack me. All I did was defend myself. It's not fair that I'm here."

"But why are you so accepting of it?"

"Because I have a district attorney who's ready to file a criminal complaint against me if I don't take this class. You have an employer who's willing to send you back to India if you don't take this class. I don't know about you, but I've worked too hard to get where I am. I'm not going to throw it all away because of pride."

Prachi sniffled. She, too, had worked hard to achieve her place in the world. And she certainly didn't want to return home under these circumstances—disgraced, ashamed. "I understand that. But how can I let him victimize me like this?"

"Who?"

"An executive vice president at the company where I work. He's the one who lied and said I threw a picture frame, which I assuredly did not. I *did* leave his office frustrated because he refused to listen to me about some test results, but I didn't throw anything."

Sasha's green eyes were thoughtful. "These test results are important, aren't they?"

Prachi hesitated, unsure of how much to say. Finally, she settled on the short and sweet truth. "Yes. It's a safety issue."

"And you think your company sent you here in an effort to keep you quiet?"

"Of course. They concocted this anger problem so I'm under a threat of deportation. They want to cow me into silence. I'm working on a time-sensitive project; I'm sure that's the only reason they haven't already fired me."

"Hmm."

Prachi chewed on her lower lip for a moment and considered whether to trust this stranger. But the reality was, there was nobody else she could tell. And something about the woman gave her comfort. She lowered her voice and confided, "I'm constructing a laboratory of my own to re-run the test. If they won't do it, I will."

"It seems they've misjudged you. You're a fighter."

Prachi bristled.

Sasha continued, "I don't mean that in a bad

way, not at all. You'll persevere to do what you think is right. Consequences be damned."

It was true, Prachi thought, although part of her wished it weren't. This woman didn't know about the trash-picking jobs, the slums she'd lived in, or how much her family had sacrificed to give her a chance. University and then a job in the United States had been the end goal her entire life —and now she was in danger of losing it all.

"I suppose so. That's what my name means —fighter."

Sasha smiled. "Great name. Well, look, I know a thing or two about being underestimated. Now, I'd prefer that you don't share what I'm about to tell you with our classmates."

She paused and waited for Prachi to nod her agreement.

"I'm an attorney."

Prachi scrunched up her face. "That's your shameful secret?"

"I'm not ashamed of it. It's just the fact that I specialize in commercial litigation. I wouldn't want Lani, Gracelyn, or Carla to think that I could help with family law or criminal issues, which it sounds as if they have—in spades. I don't say it to be unkind; it's just the reality."

"I see. But then, why are you telling me this?"

"Because I do know enough employment law to know that you likely have a whistleblower claim, as well as a retaliation claim against your employer."

"No, I don't want to sue. Surely they'll cancel my visa," she said, panicked at the mere thought of a legal battle.

"Take it easy. You may not want to file a complaint, but you need to protect yourself—particularly if you don't plan to drop your concerns about this safety issue. Retain a lawyer, just so you have someone in your corner if—more likely when—the time comes. Think of it as mutually assured destruction."

Prachi considered this. "You can help me?"

"No, I'm not qualified. And the only thing worse than representing yourself is being represented by an incompetent attorney." She removed a business card from her wallet and scrawled a name on the back. "This man specializes in employment *and* immigration law. He's very good. Call his office first thing in the morning and tell him I referred you. I'll send him an email when I get home tonight to let him know he'll be hearing from you."

"Thank you," Prachi said. The words felt insufficient. Relief that someone was finally listening, finally willing to help her, warmed her from the inside out, much like a hot mug of her mother's fragrant chai used to warm her when she wasn't feeling well as a little girl.

"Don't mention it. Come on, we'd better get back before Mrs. Hogan locks us out."

11

The crisis management consultant looked down at his cell phone display with a mixture of irritation and wonder. Although the nature of his job dictated he make a telephone number available to his clients, he took pains to impress upon them that they were not to call him after he'd been engaged to perform work unless there was a true emergency.

His explanation was sufficiently colorful, and the promised consequences sufficiently dire, that —to a man—no client had ever called. Until now.

"Yes?" he answered in a clipped tone, devoid of emotion.

"We have a problem." Charles Merriman

endeavored to keep the emotion out of his voice, as well, but with no success.

"I'm taking care of *your* problem," he assured the man, placing slight emphasis to remind him that they didn't share ownership of the problem— or anything else for that matter.

"No, you don't understand—"

"The process is underway. The attorney is being neutralized. The wheels are in motion; you just need to sit back and be patient."

"No, there's a new wrinkle," Merriman insisted. "Something else has popped up. I need you to help out with it."

The consultant bristled. He wasn't a cleanup crew. He considered himself a surgeon—a precision operator, not a generalist. "Is this new problem related to my work for you?"

"No. Well, yes. I suppose it depends on how you look at it. This issue could jeopardize the transaction that we hired you to protect from that ... other situation."

The consultant waited for him to finish hemming and hawing. "Is this problem related to the arbitration?"

"Not exactly. But it is related to the subject matter of the arbitration."

The consultant considered this. He was a great believer in the saying 'pigs get fed; hogs get slaughtered.' He strove for complete satisfaction and would not ordinarily charge for any ancillary work that came up after he was engaged by a client. At the same time, unlike most service providers, he wasn't interested in repeat business—it was simply too risky. He liked to get in, get the job done, and get out. Never to be contacted again. And yet, if this new issue could undermine his work, that wouldn't do.

Finally, his mind made up, he said, "I'm willing to discuss entering into a second, separate arrangement to handle this new issue. The compensation terms would be the same, including a new retainer."

His listened for pushback. Pushback would mean this wasn't as big of a problem as the client wanted him to believe—maybe the man was just looking for a freebie. It was, after all, the American way. But no pushback came.

"Of course. Whatever you need. I'll arrange for the wire transfer. When can we meet? There's some urgency here. We have a rogue employee who—"

"Not over the phone." It was almost as though

he didn't counsel his clients about proper precautions at the outset, he thought with disdain. He checked his calendar app on the phone. "Tonight. Seven p.m."

"The same place?"

No. It was never the same place. He rattled off the address of a different hotel bar. It would have the same overpriced cocktail menu, the same interchangeable leather furniture, and identical dim lighting as the spot where they'd met before. But the bartenders, waiters, and valets —the people whose tips depended on remembering names, faces, and preferences—would be different. He ended the call and returned to the lap blanket he'd been crocheting when the phone had rung. He picked up his hook, counted his stitches, and found his place. The purple metallic hook flashed in his hand, fast and precise. He wielded a size H crochet hook with the same level of skill as he did his seven-inch tactical knife.

12

Leo jerked his head away from his laptop screen and toward the hallway at the sound of the *snick*. It was the sound of the front door lock turning. He glanced at the time displayed on his computer to confirm that it was only four in the afternoon. Then he saved his work and powered down. He hadn't expected to see Sasha until seven tonight at the earliest. He padded barefoot to the front of the house to greet her.

"They're both napping," he stage whispered.

She turned from the entryway closet, where she was stowing her bag, and gave him a smile. "How long have they been down?"

"About twenty minutes. They had a pretty big day."

"Music and movement class, right?" she asked as she wriggled her feet out of her heels and tossed them in the general direction of the staircase.

"Right. And we stopped at the park afterward. They should be tired out."

He resisted the urge to instantly go straighten the shoes. An unexpected Sasha appearance in the middle of the day while the twins were sleeping was a rare bonus. He could think of several other things he'd rather do with her than tidy up her messes.

"That makes three of us."

"What's the occasion—did you climb out your window and sneak away?"

She laughed, but he could tell her heart wasn't in it.

"Not exactly. I just needed some air so I took a walk around the block, and well ... I guess I just kept walking." She stretched up onto the tips of her toes and planted a kiss on his chin, and then she walked toward the kitchen.

He followed her and watched as she filled a glass with water. "I thought you were busy getting ready for that arbitration that's coming up."

"I was. But now I'm not."

"Why?"

"Because I'm off the case." She drank the entire glass of water in one long gulp and rested the glass on the counter beside the sink.

"We don't have to talk about it if you don't want to."

"It's not that I don't want to talk about it but there's nothing to talk about. It's the client's call."

Her words were matter-of-fact, but her voice shook with emotion. He wrinkled his forehead in confusion.

"I don't understand. They've been so happy with your work. Why would they remove you from the arbitration team?"

"The optics. It wouldn't look good for them to be represented in a complex commercial arbitration matter by a brawler."

"Pardon?" he asked, certain he'd misheard her.

"The bar fight, Connelly. Somebody sent them a clipping from the *Pittsburgh Legal Journal* about my arrest."

A shock of anger coursed through him. "Who would do that? And why?"

She shrugged at the indignation in his voice. "It's not worth getting mad about. I'm sure it came from opposing counsel's office—or from someone at the target company. Pretty much any lawyer worth his salt would have done it. I might have myself if the shoe were on the other foot."

He stared at her. "Would you really?"

"Maybe. An attorney's supposed to zealously represent her client. If an advantage falls into my lap, I'd be remiss if I didn't capitalize on it. And my bad luck is a godsend for them. I have them dead to rights, and everyone involved knows it."

"So how does this help them—won't Naya or Will just step in and take over?"

"They sure will."

He shook his head. "Then what's the point?"

"Well, what they actually wanted was a postponement. The same day my client received the clipping in the mail, counsel for Playtime Toys called and suggested that the parties delay the arbitration. He said, given my situation, they were willing to agree to a postponement of a month or two. By then, this would have all blown over and wouldn't be a distraction."

"That's true, though, right? So why not just postpone the arbitration until after you finish ARD? Especially if the other side is going to be so gracious about it?"

She looked at him in amazement. "There's nothing remotely gracious about the offer. They want us to agree to a delay because it would give them time finish the database, which, in turn, would obviate our claim that time is of the essence for the delivery of a fully-populated and functioning database. Or, even better, they still wouldn't finish the database, but we'd pay the full price and have to go after them for a refund, which defeats the purpose of the pre-closing arbitration in the first place. They want us to close the transaction without getting what we paid for. They're selling us a pig in a poke."

He was getting a headache from trying to discern all the maneuvers and counter-maneuvers at play, and his hopes for an afternoon frolic and detour were evaporating.

He gave her a long look. "Your client was willing to agree to the postponement, weren't they?"

She pulled a face but didn't answer.

He continued, "This mess has all the hallmarks of your finely developed sense of right and wrong. You decided, on principle, that it would be better for you to step aside than to let Playtime Toys gain a tactical advantage, didn't you?"

Her pursed lips turned upward into a faint, rueful smile. "Something like that," she admitted.

"That's why you're so frustrated. You were hoisted by your own petard. The only person you can be mad at is yourself."

"Okay, fine. You know me so well. Will said the same thing. But the fact that I fenced myself in doesn't make it any less aggravating. This whole thing is all my fault."

"How so?"

"Well, for starters, I was helping Naya with the due diligence review. But I'm not a transactional lawyer. I didn't realize that one of the intangible assets they gave us was basically garbage. I didn't know what I was looking at."

"But they more or less lied, right? I mean, isn't that what the arbitration's about? That's not your fault."

She blew out a breath. "Yeah. But then, this whole criminal mess came along. If I hadn't stepped in to take care of that jerk in the bar—"

"Stop right there. It may be true that no good deed goes unpunished, but that doesn't mean we stop doing them," he cut her off.

She was leaning against the counter. He moved in front of her, rested his hands on the counter with her in the middle, and covered her lips with a long kiss. When he pulled back, he searched her face. "Why don't you give Daniel a call? I'm sure a session of sparring and hand-to-hand combat would help you clear your head and work out some aggression."

Her green eyes pierced him. "I'm sure it would. But I was thinking of a different kind of one-on-one session to clear my head." She raised her eyebrows and glanced toward the stairs.

"Oh, yeah?"

In answer, she slipped her hand into his and led him out of the kitchen.

13

The consultant leaned back and rested his head against the soft leather of the chair. He watched Charles Merriman's face. His client was definitely panicking and possibly lying. The first condition wasn't troubling —many of his clients were in freak-out mode by the time they involved him. The second condition was highly problematic.

"Do you understand what I'm saying?" Merriman demanded.

The consultant gave him a hard look before answering. "It's not hard to follow. You have some scientist who believes one of your products is defective. Your management folks disagree. This is not the sort of thing you need me for. Just fire him."

Merriman clucked in exasperation. The consultant noted that he sounded just like a chicken.

"First of all, it's a she—some lady scientist from India. And we can't just fire her. She's building the database we need to hand over to Recreation Group, Inc. as part of the sale of the business. Nobody else can populate it as quickly as she can. As you know, we can't meet the deadline as it is—hence, your work for us."

A wrinkle. But not a wrinkle that merited calling him. "So, tell her you're looking into her concerns. Glad-hand her. Then bury her report." This was basic management stuff. How had this guy gotten this far in the business world without figuring any of this out?

Another cluck. "We've done all that, and more. One of the vice presidents ginned up a complaint about her. Human resources called her in. She's on probation, attending anger management classes under the threat of deportation if she screws up again. She should be falling into line."

The consultant nodded, mildly impressed with

their efforts despite himself. "So what's the problem?"

"She's not falling into line. Our security system caught her on video sneaking into a storage room in a part of the building she had no reason to be in. She came out minutes later with something under her lab coat."

"Maybe she's stealing pens."

"She's not stealing pens. We inventoried the room. Three packages are missing. It's the product she sounded the alarm about."

"She stole it?"

"She took it without permission. I need to know why."

"So ask her."

"It's not that simple."

The consultant crossed his arms. "It is that simple if the product isn't defective. Did you forget to tell me something?"

Merriman fell silent, tracing a finger over the gilt script embossed into to the leather cover of the cocktail menu. Then he sighed. "This is complicated. It's not that the product's defective. It works the way it's supposed to. It's just that we're required by a federal statute to send it out to a third party to test the levels of a bunch of heavy metals."

"Why?"

"Because we make toys, and children have a tendency to put things in their mouths. And if those things contain high levels of lead or arsenic, for example, it's not good for their health."

"You're selling children's toys that contain unsafe levels of arsenic?" Maybe he had misjudged the man.

"No, of course not. Our products are safe, made in the United States from natural materials. That's a big reason Recreation Group wants to buy us— our reputation is stellar. But this product—one batch of it, to be precise—came back with unusual testing results. Out of the blue, we had a sample show high levels of mercury. She sounded the alarm."

"I need you to level with me. Is this product unsafe?"

The CEO gulped. "No, of course not."

He couldn't be sure if the man was lying or just worried. "So retest it."

"We can't."

"What do you mean, you can't?"

"Well, we *could*. But it's expensive and time-consuming. It's a distraction we don't need, not now with the sale. And if we send the samples back to the lab, we create a trail. We could come under fire for not recalling the product from the market until we get it sorted. And a recall would be a public relations nightmare."

"And it would impair your value. I imagine Recreation Group would want to lower the purchase price."

"I imagine so," Merriman said grimly. "We're a rarity in the industry because we've never recalled a product."

"So, you want to just let these little kids eat mercury and die?"

The client jerked back as if he'd been slapped. "Of course not. We're confident the testing results were flawed. The product is safe. We just can't spare the expense and time to prove it right now. But we don't need to."

"What do you mean, you don't need to? You just said you're required by law to test the stuff."

Merriman leaned forward with an excited gleam in his eyes. "My regulatory people tell me the product in question is currently categorized as a children's toy, but, with a few keystrokes we can re-categorize it as an art supply, which isn't subject to the same heavy metals testing. Problem solved."

"Part of the problem. Your regulatory suits can't

muzzle the scientist. If she's willing to risk deportation, you're well and truly screwed."

"That's where you come in."

The consultant mulled it over. "I could silence her permanently, but that would mean your database deadline slips."

Fear filled the CEO's eyes. "No, no, nothing like that. I was hoping you could somehow convince her to be quiet since the threat of deportation doesn't seem to have done the trick. You know, just temporarily apply some pressure—like you did with the attorney."

"Ah, so Recreation Group agreed to postpone the hearing?" He'd put the wheels into motion by mailing the news item, but he hadn't yet heard if the plan had worked. He was pleased that it had come to fruition so quickly.

"Well, not exactly. But they removed her from the matter. It's not as good—but it should slow them down."

His pleasure morphed instantly into rage. "No. You hired me to secure a postponement. You'll get your postponement. Don't worry."

He pressed his palms down flat on the table to stop himself from making a fist. He prided himself on not showing anger. Anger was an emotion of weakness. He wouldn't reveal it to a client, but it roiled inside him. He'd have to come at the attorney from another angle. He exhaled.

"Of course. But this other matter?"

"I have an idea."

"She won't be ... put out of commission, correct?"

"Correct."

Merriman's tanned face relaxed and he raised his martini in a salute. "Wonderful."

"Don't start celebrating yet. I have a question. If you lie to me, our business relationship is over. And believe me, I'll know if you lie."

Merriman bobbed his head, wide-eyed. "I understand."

"Is this the first time you've got bad test results back—on any product, for any reason?"

Merriman tried to hold his gaze, but his eyes ended up on the table. "No," he mumbled.

"Good. I just want to know what kind of man I'm dealing with." He finished his drink and walked away. Merriman could buy this round.

14

Sasha took one look at Will and Naya's matching expressions of doom, and her stomach plunged.

"What?" she demanded.

Naya glanced at Will for guidance. He reached behind him and closed Sasha's office door. Not good.

"Seriously—spit it out."

"Why don't we go to Jake's and get a coffee," Will suggested. "Or maybe to that Tex-Mex place you two like. We can talk over margaritas."

Sasha dropped her pen on her desk and leaned forward. "When Will proposes cocktails at eleven-forty on a Monday morning, it doesn't give me comfort. Can you two please just tell me what's wrong?"

Naya dropped heavily into one of Sasha's guest chairs. Will stood behind the other, gripping the back. "I got a call from our former place of employment."

"Ugh. What do they want?"

Another furtive look passed between Naya and Will.

"It was a courtesy call. Although, honestly, it perverts the meaning of the word 'courtesy' to apply it to this situation."

"Will," Sasha warned. She was losing her patience.

Naya blurted it out. "Kevin Marcus is emailing over a draft complaint against you."

"Against me?"

"You, personally. He's been retained by Steve Harold."

Sasha tossed her head like Mocha trying to shake the water off his ears after a bath. "Pardon? The man from the bar?"

"The one and only," Will said wryly.

"And he's suing me for ... what exactly?"

"I haven't seen the complaint yet, but from

what Kevin said it's basically an emotional distress claim."

"Oh, come on!" She shot out of her chair.

"Take it easy, Mac," Naya urged her.

"This is beyond the pale."

"It is," Will agreed.

She paced around her office like a caged feline. "So, it's a hold up? He's just looking for a settlement, right?"

Naya wet her lips to answer but Will beat her to it. "It's a hold up, that much is certain. But Kevin says they'll be seeking damages from the firm itself."

"What? On what basis?" Sasha exploded. She knew she was yelling. There was no doubt she could be heard in the reception area. But she didn't give a flying fig.

"No basis. It's blackmail, pure and simple. But they must mean it. Why else would Kevin Marcus be involved?" Naya answered.

Marcus had run Prescott & Talbott's litigation group for a solid decade. He didn't make it a practice to waste his time. Sasha let out a great *whoosh* of breath. "Well, I'd like to see him file it. It'll get kicked on a demurrer. And I'm going to research possible misconduct charges against Prescott. And counterclaims against that weasel Harold. Does the district attorney's office know about this?" She shook with pent-up rage.

Another knowing look flew from Will to Naya.

"Stop communicating through secret glances," she snapped.

"Sasha, we're going to have to put you on leave, just until this blows over," Will finally said. "Think of it as a paid sabbatical. Take a vacation, maybe."

*Leave? They were trying to kick her out the door of the firm **she** started? The hell they were.*

She cocked her head and gave him an icy look. Then she turned to Naya and let her have the death glare, too. "I don't need a vacation. Besides, I can't go anywhere. I can't miss my *anger management class*," she hissed.

"It's for your own protection," he tried.

"Will, no—"

"And ours," Naya added in a soft voice. "You have to think about what's best for the firm, Mac. I know it's not fair. It sucks. But people depend on you for their livelihoods. It's for the best. We ran it by the malpractice carrier."

The feeling of betrayal smacked her in the face like a fist. "How are you going to manage my caseload and yours?" she mumbled.

"We'll split things up and ask for extensions where necessary," Will assured her.

She fixed him with a look. "But not on the Recreation Group arbitration, right? I mean, that case is teed up. All you have to do is show up and argue."

He sighed. "I'm not you, Sasha. I don't have the familiarity with the issues that you do. Without you here to answer questions and take over some of my workload, it's just not feasible to keep the hearing date. We'll do the hearing post-closing. The client understands."

"That's a terrible plan," she told him.

"But it's not your call to make," he said in a soft voice.

No, she supposed it wasn't. She stared down at her feet, reeling from what had just happened.

"Sasha?"

She didn't respond.

"Are you okay, Mac?"

"Call Connelly, please," she finally said, still looking down at the floor through a watery blur.

LEO WATCHED his wife as she pushed Finn and Fiona on the tire swing. She smiled at each squeal of excitement that rose up from the swing, and her face gave no hint of hidden strain. And yet, Leo knew she had to be distracted, thinking about her conversation with Will and Naya.

It was not in Sasha's nature to go with the flow —not in her daily life and not in the aftermath of a crisis. In an actual high-stakes emergency, sure, she was preternaturally calm. During closing arguments in a big case or when she was literally physically taking down a bad guy, she was all steely nerves and complete focus.

It was afterward, once the adrenaline rush had dissipated and reality set in, when she shut down. She retreated into herself—not eating, not talking. She would sleep for hours, all day if he let her, which was ironic considering she rarely got more than four or five hours of sleep—and it was interrupted sleep, at that.

Maybe, he thought, she's reacting differently because now the kids were old enough to sense if she was upset.

"Whee!" Finn shouted as he circled by in a blur.

"Faster, faster!" Fiona called.

Leo caught Sasha's eye. "Don't get carried away. She's a complete speed demon," he called in warning.

"I can't believe I get to be the one to tell you to relax for a change." She laughed at him, and he had to admit her amusement sounded genuine.

He gave Mocha's leash a tug to get him moving. He'd been smelling the same bush in the mulch bed for the past eight minutes. Mocha gave the bush one last baleful sniff before trotting along beside him.

He walked over to the swing set. She shielded her eyes from the afternoon sun and looked up at him.

"Are you okay?" he asked in a low voice. "I mean, really, truly okay?" He kept his tone light but looked at her steadily to make sure she understood he wanted the absolute truth.

She answered in a soft voice with her attention on the swing. "I'm as okay as I can be. It's not my decision to make, and it's not the decision I would have made. But Will and Naya are just thinking of the firm."

The words came out robotically like a poem someone had asked elementary school students to memorize without explaining the meaning.

"Sasha—" he began.

"What am I going to do about it? I'm not worried about the actual case—it's a crap claim. I mean, sure I'm angry that Prescott would even contemplate representing that dirtbag, but mainly I'm mad that Playtime Toys is getting its postponement. But, what can I do? It's out of my hands."

He searched her face. "And how does it feel to have something out of your hands?"

He saw a flash of life in her eyes. "How do you think it feels, Connelly?" she answered, nearly spitting the words.

"Sorry. Okay. Hey, Daniel and Chris invited us to one of their swanky dinner parties this weekend. We should go. It'll cheer you up."

"We can't."

"Why?"

"My parents are going out of town, and despite Daniel and Chris's repeated assurances that kids are welcome, their place is a freaking deathtrap. It's nothing but glass and sharp corners. All they need is a barbed wire sculpture."

He laughed despite himself. The picture she drew of their childless friends' pad was scarily accurate. "But still, we can't hide."

"I'm not hiding."

Leo thought for a moment. "What about Jordana?"

"What about her?"

"She could babysit for a few hours on Friday night, right?"

Sasha was silent for just a beat. He thought for sure she was going to shoot down the idea. Then she shrugged. "I guess," she agreed without enthusiasm.

15

Prachi practically bounded up the stairs to her apartment. This was the most light-hearted she'd felt since she'd discovered the test results. *Hopeful,* she thought. *That was the feeling. She felt hope that someone was going to help her.*

She'd risked Maureen's wrath and requested a personal day—her first weekday away from Playtime Toys since she'd arrived in Pittsburgh. She'd used the time to meet with the attorney who Sasha McCandless had recommended. He'd given her great comfort. He was self-assured and made her feel as though the matter was in good hands. He would protect her so that she could do her job properly. She was sure of it.

She turned the key in her door and dumped her mail on the counter. She still had the entire afternoon free. Part of her—the diligent, well-trained part—considered going into the office to work on the database even though she wouldn't be paid for her efforts during a personal day. But she knew that setting foot inside Playtime Toys' space would dampen her mood instantly, and she wanted to prolong her happiness.

Perhaps she would take herself to a matinee movie or do some midday shopping. Tomorrow, after work, she would stay late after everyone left and run the tests on the samples. Her gaze fell on her oven and she laughed softly. After she'd taken the samples from the storage closet, she couldn't risk leaving them at work until she was ready to use them; so she'd smuggled them home. Then, on a whim, she decided to stow them in her oven. Storage space was at a premium in her postage-stamp-sized apartment, and the oven served no other purpose. Given her work hours, she hadn't turned it on in months.

She reached into her tote and pulled out the journal she'd stopped and splurged on at the bookstore. Although the lawyer had told her she could use anything—a sheet of loose-leaf paper, even a series of sticky notes—to memorialize what had happened and to start keeping contemporaneous notes, she wanted to mark the undertaking in some way to recognize its importance to her. Because it *was* important. She was living up to her name.

When she saw the beautiful writer's notebook, she was instantly drawn to its richly colored cover and its satisfying heft in her hand. Looking at it now, she was inspired to write. She sat down at her square kitchen table and uncapped her pen. Before she'd even dated her first entry, though, the image of her mother writing out letters longhand while drinking tea on their sunny patio entered her mind. A mug of tea would put her in just the right frame of mind for her task.

She hummed to herself as she filled the kettle with water. While it heated, she dried and put away her breakfast dishes, which she'd washed and left to drain before her appointment with the lawyer.

The first time she heard the noise, she dismissed it. Between the clatter of the dishes and the hissing of the kettle, the muffled bumping sound could have been anything—or nothing.

The second time, she knew it was not nothing. Someone was in her apartment.

SOMEONE WAS IN THE APARTMENT, the consultant realized with a start. He wheeled around Prachi Agarwal's tidy bedroom looking for a place to hide. The closet was miniscule—and also the first place she'd look. He bent and lifted the comforter to check under the bed. No space. Solid wood drawers lined both sides of the platform.

Think.

What was she even doing home in the middle of the day? Why wasn't she at work?

He'd planned to rifle through her possessions in search of some personal information he could use as leverage to guarantee her silence—a lover back home, a sick parent, *something*. Now he was trapped in the small apartment with her—and without a plan.

Not good.

He crept to the window and tried to raise the pane. It didn't budge. He looked more closely and noticed that the pane was caulked to the frame. Glued closed. Not very safe in the event of a fire.

Or an intruder. He tugged at it, but the caulk held. Sweat dripped from his hairline.

He was going to have to confront her. There was no other choice. He'd menace her, make some vague veiled threats about remaining silent, and leave. Less than ideal, he realized. But it would have to do for the time being. He walked stealthily toward the front of the apartment.

PRACHI GRABBED a knife from the block near the windowsill as her mind went into analytical overdrive, calculating how many hiding spots there were in the eight-hundred-square-foot space: hall closet; bathroom; behind the couch. Three possible places where an intruder could conceal himself.

Her legs trembled and her heart raced as she stalked through the small space, gripping the knife tightly. Although the sound seemed to have come from the back of the apartment, possibly her bedroom, she decided to begin her search with the hall closet because it was closest.

She tiptoed to the closet door. She could hear her heart thumping wildly. She stared at the door for a long moment, gathering her courage; yanked the doorknob with her left hand; and thrust the knife into the closet. Spare sheets, neatly folded towels, her parka, a large box of Indian spices from the spice shop in the Strip District. Otherwise, the closet was empty. She closed the door and leaned against it until her heart rate returned to normal.

As she walked into the living room space to check behind the couch, the tea kettle whistled, high and shrill. She jumped and let out a shriek of her own. Laughing at her jumpiness, she changed course and headed to the kitchen to remove the kettle from the stove. She rested the knife on the counter and turned the burner to the 'off' position.

"Were you looking for me?" a deep, male voice said behind her, so close to her ear that she could feel the speaker's breath on her neck.

Prachi froze, unwilling to turn around to see the intruder and unable to think of a way out.

He reached out his hand and snatched up the knife. "I think I'll take this."

Throw the boiling water at him, her brain finally said, breaking through the ice that seemed to encase her. *Count to three, reach for the handle, press down to open the spout, and splash. One motion, fluid and fast. You only have one chance.*

"Dr. Agarwal, I have to say, you aren't being a very good hostess."

She didn't recognize the voice. But the fact that he knew her name sent a secondary chill of terror coursing through her.

One. Two. She tried to steady her shaking hand. *Three.*

She grasped the handle as she turned and sloshed the hot water toward the stranger standing in her kitchen.

He howled and his hands flew up to cover his face. The knife clattered to the floor.

Pick it up or run?

Run.

She raced past him, making a beeline for the front door. Her trembling hands slipped off the doorknob. Tears streamed from her eyes, making it so hard to see. Behind her, the man bellowed like an enraged animal and charged at her.

She gripped the door again, turning the knob—and he threw himself at her, slamming her into the door and knocking the breath out of her. He clamped his hand around her wrist and pulled her away from the door, away from safety.

She tried to wrench away, but he was much

stronger than she. His face was red, a combination of rage and shiny burns from the water.

"I just came here to talk. You shouldn't have done that." He forced the words out from between clenched teeth.

"I'm ... I'm sorry," she sobbed.

"You will be," he growled.

"Help!" she shouted as loudly as she could, praying her voice would travel down the hallway and one of her neighbors would be home midday and willing to investigate.

The man's entire demeanor changed in a nanosecond. It was as though he flipped a switch from wild and furious to controlled. "I'm here to deliver a message. That's all."

He released her wrist and spread his hands wide in a gesture she imagined was intended to allay her fears. It did not.

"Help!" she yelled once more, more desperately this time.

"Be quiet," he thundered.

His face darkened, and the only way she could think of to describe his expression was 'murderous.' She lunged for the door again.

❧

THE CRISIS MANAGEMENT consultant sighed heavily as he looked down at the body. Things had not gone according to plan, to put it mildly. The skin on his cheeks and forehead burned, raw and hot, from the dousing with boiling water. A matching heat rose from inside his chest.

He ran through the list of mistakes and surprises, both avoidable and unavoidable, while he retraced his steps through the apartment, wiping down every surface and item he had touched. She wasn't supposed to be home in the middle of the workday. That was the principal surprise, which led like a tipped-over domino to all the mistakes that followed, one after another in a cascade that ended with Prachi Agarwal's dead body on the tile flooring between her front door and her kitchen.

Killing her had, of course, been an accident. More problematic, it was also an error. His client had been very clear about her importance to the project.

It never occurred to him to panic, though. After all, this was what he did for a living.

He lowered himself to a kitchen chair. Disposing of the body would be easily managed. Handling his client would take some finesse. He looked from the body to the bound journal lying open on the table in front of him and then back to the corpse. An idea was bubbling up in his consciousness. He closed his eyes and allowed it to fully form.

He picked up the pen and began to write. When he finished, he read it over, nodded with satisfaction. Then he mopped up the puddle of water on the kitchen floor and dried the kettle, wiped it down, and placed it on the back burner where women seemed to like to store their tea kettles when not in use. He surveyed the space with a careful eye to see if there was any stray detail that he'd overlooked.

He needed to call in a specialist for the rest of the job. But using his cell phone here, from inside her apartment, would be reckless to the point of stupidity. What option did he have? He couldn't leave a dead body lying on the floor just inside an unlocked door. And he couldn't very well lock up behind him.

He paced across the floor and tried to come up with a solution, but there was no other option. He'd just have to ensure no one ever had reason to triangulate his calls. He took out his cell phone and scrolled through his contacts to find the right contractor for this job. He settled on Dutch, a surly, nearly-mute mountain of a man from Uniontown, and placed the call.

Dutch answered on the second ring. "Aye."

"I have something for you. Disposal."

Silence on the line. "Twelve thousand."

"Rates have gone up, eh?"

"It's twelve thousand."

The consultant didn't care to dicker. "Fine." He recited the address for the cleaner and gave him instructions to park behind the building.

"How do I get in?"

"I'll let you in. Then I'm leaving."

He wasn't squeamish by nature, but Dutch's methods were both thorough and brutal. It wasn't a show he particularly wanted to watch. He ended the call and squatted by the body. *Damn you, Prachi Agarwal. Why did you come home so early?*

Although he knew Dutch was meticulous, he nonetheless removed the woman's jewelry. There was no reason not to take every possible step to inhibit identification, just in case Dutch missed something. He checked the pockets of her flat-fronted trousers. The left pocket was empty. From the right, he fished out a business card. He stared down at the spare, modern typeface, not believing his eyes: *Sasha McCandless-Connelly, Partner, McCandless & Volmer.*

He thought back to a Chinese saying a client had once shared with him: No coincidence, no story.

His client's point had been that human beings are hard-wired to seek meaning in events, but sometimes a coincidence was just a coincidence with no serendipitous or universal message. He agreed with the argument. But, at this moment, this specific coincidence seemed rife with import. He slipped the card into his wallet, pointedly ignoring the faint hint of a tremor that barely shook his fingers.

16

Sasha squirmed in her desk chair, her eyes ping-ponging between the classroom door and the large, gray institutional-style clock on the wall above the whiteboard. Although Karen Hogan had already entered the classroom, closed the door, and begun to write the day's exercises on the whiteboard, it wasn't yet quite six o'clock. So, technically, anyone who came into the room in the next ninety seconds, give or take, wouldn't be tardy.

Sasha shifted her attention to the empty seat on the other side of the circle. Carla, Gracelyn, and Lani seemed unperturbed by their classmate's absence. Truthfully, Sasha was surprised at her own level of concern.

The clock ticked loudly. The minute hand jittered and jumped to the twelve. Karen Hogan's wristwatch beeped. She capped her dry erase marker, checked the wall clock, and gave a little cluck—whether of disapproval or disappointment, Sasha couldn't tell. "Well, ladies, it appears we're down to four."

Without further preamble, she began to explain their first assignment of the night—a role-playing exercise designed to teach them how to empathize with other points of view. Sasha dragged her eyes away from the door and pulled her desk across from Gracelyn's, at Karen Hogan's direction.

As Sasha and Gracelyn took turns being the boss in a far-fetched scenario that made clear Karen Hogan had never worked in retail, Sasha paid only partial attention. Most of her energy was devoted to wondering what would've caused Prachi to miss the class she needed in order to stay in the United States and fight her company's bad behavior.

"Sasha? Sasha!" Gracelyn's voice cut through her musing.

She pulled her attention back to the classroom and her partner.

"Sorry. My mind wandered for a minute there. Can you repeat yourself, please?"

Gracelyn gave her a put-upon look. "I said we've gone through the whole list, and Carla and Lani are already done."

"Oh. Okay."

Gracelyn stared at her. "Mrs. Hogan said we could take our break early tonight, but you're a million miles away. You're not coming down with anything, are you? I don't have any sick days left—I can't miss work."

"I'm just a little distracted," she promised.

She stood and waited while the others gathered up their cigarettes and cell phones and filed out of the classroom. Karen Hogan sat behind the metal desk at the front of the room and flipped through the pages of some sort of manual. As Sasha approached, she marked her place with her finger and looked up.

"Can I help you with something, Sasha?"

"I was wondering if you knew anything about Dr. Agarwal's absence."

Karen pressed her lips into a thin line. "I know all I need to know. She missed class. She's out of the program. It's a simple as that."

"Right, sure. I just wanted to know if she

contacted you—is she ill or was there some sort of emergency?"

The social worker's face softened momentarily. "It's clear that you've become friendly with Prachi. While I encourage my students to form relationships so you can provide continuing support for each other after the class ends, the reality is that not everyone who takes this class is fully committed to it. Sadly, the dropout rate is fairly high."

"I don't think she would have dropped out. She had a lot of reasons why she really needed to complete this course," Sasha tried to explain.

Mrs. Hogan shook her head sadly. "I've been teaching this course for years, Sasha. I can tell you that Prachi Agarwal was not dedicated to working on her anger issues; she was still in the habit of blaming others for her behavior. I've seen it many times before. One day, she may reach a place where she's ready to do the work, until then ... well, it's best not to get attached."

Sasha gave the woman a blank look. She had obviously made up her mind about Prachi, so continuing to argue was pointless. Besides, it sounded like Karen Hogan didn't know why Prachi had missed class, anyway.

After a moment, she pasted an agreeable smile on her face and said, "You'd know best. But, as you said, I did become friendly with Prachi. I don't suppose you have a telephone number for her? Or perhaps you could give me her email address?"

"I'm afraid that's not possible. To the extent she wanted to, she was, of course, free to share that information with her classmates; but it would be a violation of privacy law for me to do so."

Sasha cocked her head, trying to figure out what possible privacy regulations a court-certified anger management class fell under. Educational privacy law? HIPAA? Or was Karen Hogan making it up to seem important?

"You could make an exception, just this once," Sasha suggested.

"Absolutely not. Now, the break is already half over. I suggest you avail yourself of the time that remains. I'm going to use the restroom before class resumes."

"Okay," Sasha said meekly. She watched as the woman closed up her book and placed it beside her large teacher's course agenda. "I suppose you're right about Prachi."

The social worker gave her a knowing smile. "I'm certain I am."

They walked together toward the door. Sasha waited until Karen was already through the doorway and several feet down the hallway. Then she stopped in her tracks and said, "Oh, I forgot my cell phone. I need to call and check on my kids. I'll just run back and get it."

Mrs. Hogan clicked her tongue. "You make sure you close the door behind you, and don't be late coming back from the break."

"Yes, ma'am," Sasha said.

Mrs. Hogan turned and click-clacked down the hallway to the restroom. The sound of her sensible shoes striking the tile echoed as she moved along the corridor. Sasha started back inside and headed straight for Karen's desk and her planner. She flipped through the pages until she found the class roster. A telephone number was listed beside Prachi Agarwal's name. She committed the digits to memory and was about to close the book when she noticed the far right column, labeled 'referred by.' In Prachi's row, a handwritten notation read *Playtime Toys Human Resources—M. Glassman.'*

Sasha's heart rocketed into her throat. She slammed the planner closed and hurried through the door out to the hallway. She rounded the corner and pushed through the door to the vending machine room. She hurled herself into the same chair in which she'd found Prachi crying exactly one week earlier.

Playtime Toys? Prachi worked for the company that Recreation Group was planning to acquire? The very same company she had filed an arbitration claim against? She tried to convince herself it was all a coincidence, but the goosebumps rising on her arms said otherwise.

SASHA SMILED her way through dinner with Connelly and the twins, but her mind was racing a trillion miles a second. After they finished eating, Connelly cleaned up the kitchen and washed the dishes while Sasha bathed the twins. As was customary for pasta night, both Finn and Fiona had magically managed to get red sauce on parts of their bodies ranging from the backs of their knees to their armpits and the spaces behind their ears. She scrubbed away the evidence of dinner while they splashed around, playing a game that involved pirates, piranhas, and a manatee superhero.

Once they were dried and dressed in pajamas,

they wandered into their shared bedroom to continue their adventure on land. She headed down the stairs in search of Connelly and ran into him on the staircase.

"Is the great marinara sauce massacre of 2017 but a distant memory?" he asked.

"The water ran red," she replied with the hint of a smile.

He handed her a wineglass. "Want to finish off the Chianti while they finish off their game?"

She followed him back up the stairs to the little sitting room they'd created between their bedroom and the nursery. They'd positioned a small love seat at an angle that provided a good vantage point to both watch the sunset through the window over the stairs and see into the kids' room.

"You were quiet at dinner tonight," Connelly observed.

"Was I? I guess I was thinking."

"I know you were thinking. You were doing that crinkle thing with your forehead. Were you thinking about the firm?"

"No," she answered honestly as she ran her fingers across her brow to smooth it as if that would remove the furrow. "I was thinking about my anger management class."

"Really? You mean what you learned?"

"No," she snorted at the idea. "One of the women—Prachi Agarwal—didn't show up tonight. That means she'll be kicked out of the program. Since she's here on an H-1B visa, she's going to be fired and deported. I can't believe she'd let that happen."

"Wow. That's harsh. But, Sasha, you know, not everyone is as organized as you."

"She's got a Ph.D. in chemistry or computers, maybe both. I'm pretty sure she could manage to add a repeating event to her calendar for eight weeks."

He frowned. "Where are you going with this, exactly?"

She sipped her wine. "I'm worried something bad has happened to her."

"I think you're letting your imagination get the better of you. It's understandable; you must be understimulated spending your day doing puppet shows and building castles out of magnetic tiles instead of crafting cutting edge legal arguments, but—"

"Actually, I've loved being home with the twins. That's not it at all. I talked to her last week during our break. She insisted her company trumped up a disciplinary infraction against her."

"Why would they go through all the trouble to bring her over here as a skilled worker in high demand and then set her up?" he asked.

"I know, it's paranoid. But she said she uncovered something at the company—a bad test result of some sort, maybe a safety violation. When she took it to management, they told her to let it go. She persisted, and, the next thing she knew, she was on probation and being required to take an anger management class to keep her job."

"Okay, that's really bad. She still shouldn't have missed class, though, knowing what the consequences would be."

"There's more, Connelly."

He gave her a look that said 'of course, there is.' "Why am I not surprised?"

"I referred her to Mickey Collins."

"Mickey, the plaintiff's attorney?"

"He also does some employment law, and he has a few associates doing immigration work. I thought he might be able to help her."

"Okay, so you tried to help her. You aren't responsible for a perfect stranger's failure to come to class."

"I know. But it just feels wrong." She took a deep breath before going on. "Then today I found out that she works at Playtime Toys." She paused meaningfully to let the information sink in.

He waved his hand in the direction of the nursery. "It rings a bell. I think we have some of their blocks. And maybe a train set?"

"No. The reason you recognize the name is because Playtime Toys is the company that Recreation Group is buying."

He turned to face her. "The company you're arbitrating against?"

"Right. And they just happen to have an employee taking the same anger management class as me?"

"Coincidences do happen," he pointed out.

"That's a pretty big one. And now she's gone missing."

"Wait. Failing to show up for a class she doesn't think she should be required to take in the first place isn't exactly *going missing*," he said in a tone of voice she recognized as an effort to slow her down before she jumped to conclusions.

"It gives me a bad feeling, Connelly."

He searched her face. Whatever he saw must

have convinced him not to try to cajole her out of it. "Okay. What are you going to do about it?"

"The first thing I'm going to do is talk to Will and Naya. Then I'm going to use my ample free time to poke around and see if I can figure out what's going on."

"I'd tell you not to, but I know that's pointless. So let me just remind you that the last time you stepped in to help someone who didn't ask you to, it didn't end so well."

His words stung, and she wanted to shoot back with a quick retort, but, unfortunately, everything he said was true.

"I hear you. I'll be careful," she promised.

She snuggled into his side, and they finished their wine in silence, watching the twins entertain each other through the open door. She wished she could say her mind was at ease now that she'd unburdened herself by talking to her husband. But a new worry was spooling through her brain—did they have Playtime Toys in their toy box? Were they safe? Or was she unwittingly endangering her own children?

She waited until Connelly led the kids into the bathroom to brush their budding teeth. Then she plopped down on the playroom floor and began combing through the toys, sorting them into piles, searching for Playtime Toys' name on the bottom of a truck or a block, trying to weed out any danger lurking in their cozy house.

17

"Hello?" Charles Merriman's voice was heavy. Not groggy, as if the ringing cell phone had awoken him from sleep, but thick and tired, as if he'd already switched off his workday persona and was relaxing with a book or movie, winding down before bed.

The crisis management consultant had worked with the titans of industry long enough to know that when they called him, it was an urgent emergency, but when he was the one calling, it was an intrusion—particularly when the call came outside regular business hours.

"I'm terribly sorry to bother you at this hour," he said smoothly, "but you need to know that there's a situation involving your scientist."

"Oh? Do we need to meet?" Merriman was instantly alert.

The consultant paused. Ordinarily, he liked to conduct all business face-to-face. In this case, however, given that he planned to tell his client a series of bare lies, he didn't see any benefit to doing so in person. And, given the substance of his lies, in the unlikely event that someone was monitoring the CEO's telephone calls, it wouldn't bother him to spread misinformation.

"Considering the circumstances, I don't think we can wait to arrange a time to speak in person."

"What is it?"

"I was at her apartment today. She wasn't home."

"Hmm. I was told by our human resources director today that she had requested a personal day, which was notable, as it's the first day she's taken off. Perhaps she took a short trip."

"If she went away, she certainly left in a hurry."

"How could you tell?"

"Her door was unlocked, so I let myself in," he lied easily. "Nothing appeared to be out of place, except ..." He trailed off, baiting the hook.

"What?" Merriman bit.

"She left a note."

"A note? To whom?"

"It wasn't addressed to anyone in particular. There was a journal or notebook lying open in her kitchen. She'd written a message. The gist of it was that she was terribly sorry to have disappointed her family, and she couldn't face the prospect of returning home to India in shame. I'll be honest, Charles. It read to me like a suicide note."

On the other end of the phone, the CEO wheezed. "She killed herself?"

"I can't say for sure. As I said, the apartment was empty. But the wording had a finality to it."

"But, suicide. That's ... unthinkable."

"There's a certain logic to it, unfortunately. It seems the threat of deportation weighed heavily on her. It may simply have been too stressful for her to bear." He lowered his voice to a mournful note. He didn't want to go so far as to directly blame Prachi Agarwal's disappearance and suspected death on the company.

Merriman quickly connected the dots on his own. "This is terrible; human resources shouldn't have pushed her so hard."

He murmured an agreement.

Merriman went on. "Luckily, it turns out the

database is no longer important. Excellent timing, actually."

The consultant swatted aside his surprise. Of course, the database was Merriman's concern. Most corporate wrongdoing was, at its core, a function of greed, not evil. He, of all people, should know that by now.

"Oh? How's that?"

"I learned today that Recreation Group has reconsidered. They've agreed to push back the arbitration until after the sale closes," Merriman said with barely controlled glee, Prachi Agarwal's fate all but forgotten.

"Interesting. Did they say why?"

"No. I assume it was the result of some machination of yours."

"As do I," the consultant agreed. Then he returned to the subject of the scientist. "Now if Dr. Agarwal doesn't turn up in the next day or two, you should have human resources call the police."

"Oh, yes. Of course."

"Also, talk to your immigration specialists. You may need to start the process to alert Immigration and Customs Enforcement about a missing foreign national."

He had no qualms about the Department of

Homeland Security poking around. Unless Dutch fell down on the job, which was so unlikely as to be impossible, they wouldn't find anything in Prachi's apartment to trace back to him. And her body would never turn up. The feds would be chasing their tails for years.

"I'll do that in the morning."

"Unless she shows up for work, of course," the consultant added.

"Of course."

He ended the call. He should have felt satisfied. His brilliant idea to have Harold sue the lawyer had solved Merriman's problem and his own. Instead, the tight rock lodged on his chest was growing. Why did Prachi Agarwal have Sasha McCandless-Connelly's business card in her pocket?

18

Sasha had been sitting at her favorite table at Jake's since the coffee shop opened its doors at six AM—nearly two hours ago. By now, she'd drunk far too much coffee—even for her admittedly high consumption levels—and was tapping her foot nervously under the table as she stared at the doorway, waiting for Will or Naya to walk by en route to the office.

Will arrived first. He passed by in a hurry and started up the stairway to their law firm on the second floor. She stood and called his name. He turned and looked at her in surprise.

"What are you doing here?" he asked as he walked toward her.

She met him in the doorway and answered in a low voice, "I know you asked me not to come into the office, but I need to talk to you—Naya, too. When she gets here, I'll buy you both a cup of coffee."

"She's out in Stowe Township taking a witness statement this morning. You're stuck with me. Let me drop off my briefcase and tell Caroline where I'll be. I'll be back down in a few minutes."

"I'll order your morning latte for you."

He headed for the stairs, and she went to the counter to place his order. While she waited for him to return, she gathered her thoughts. It was important that she not sound like a wild-eyed conspiracy theorist because she needed him to take her seriously. She closed her eyes to do a quick breathing meditation for focus; when she opened them, Will was sitting across from her.

"Wow, you're sneakily quiet," she said.

"You must have been deep in concentration."

She gave him a sheepish shrug. "I was doing a meditation for focus, trying to think of the best way to convince you that what I'm about to tell you is critically important."

"You and I have known each other for a long

time, Sasha. We're partners, for crying aloud. I obviously trust your judgment—the current situation notwithstanding. You don't have to craft an appellate argument for me. As Naya would say, spit it out."

Here goes nothing, she thought.

"Okay. I met a woman in my anger management class. She mentioned that she was on probation at work and said she'd found a problem—a safety problem. When she brought it to the company's attention, instead of addressing the issue, they trumped up a disciplinary infraction against her."

He frowned. "If true, that's terrible."

"I have no reason to disbelieve her."

"She likely has a retaliation claim," he mused. "But if you're suggesting that the firm offer to represent her, I don't think—"

"No. I mean, I agree she has a claim, but I referred her to Mickey Collins."

"Ah, yes, good. This sort of thing would be in his wheelhouse." Will nodded and sipped his latte.

"Right. But yesterday, she didn't show up for class. And she's in the country on a skilled worker visa. So now she's not only going to be kicked out of the program, she's most likely going to be deported."

He shook his head. "That's unfortunate."

"There's no way she would've voluntarily missed class."

"She could have gotten ill or been in an accident."

"Sure, emergencies happen," she agreed. "I asked our facilitator for her contact information so I could check on her." She paused. She knew Will wouldn't approve of her snooping through Karen Hogan's papers, so she glossed over the bit about her self-help. "And it turns out that Prachi Agarwal works for Playtime Toys."

Will frowned. "That's odd."

"It's more than odd. We have to tell Recreation Group."

"Now, wait a minute—"

"They make toys. If this safety issue has to do with their products …"

"Does it?"

She hesitated. "I don't know. But we have to find out. Dr. Agarwal said something about a bad test. That sounds like a product issue, doesn't it?"

"Maybe. Not necessarily."

"We have a duty to tell our client."

She watched him as he considered it. Finally, he said, "We can't ask Naya to take this to Recreation Group. It's unsubstantiated."

"So substantiate it. Send them a set of interrogatories or a document request asking for an updated list of their testing results. They have a duty to amend the materials they've provided."

"I'm aware of their obligations. But surely you know what their position will be—responding to supplemental requests that will be answered in the ordinary course when they turn over the database is just a distraction from their work, which is already delayed. We'll end up with an even longer postponement."

"So what, then? We just stay quiet and let Recreation Group buy a potential headache?"

He took a long drink of coffee. "You have a lot of time on your hands at the moment. And an active imagination."

She began to blurt out a protest but he kept speaking.

"Sasha, I hear what you're saying. And believe me, I share your concerns. But this is a sticky situation." He gave her a long look. "It would solve a lot of problems if Prachi Agarwal turned up and felt like talking. I'm sorry, Sasha, but I have to run. Thanks for the coffee."

As she watched him leave, her chest was heavy with disappointment, but the wheels were beginning to turn. Prachi Agarwal would just have to turn up, then.

19

"Good morning. You've reached the Law Offices of McCandless & Volmer. How may I direct your call?" the pleasant, polished voice answered.

"Yes, I'm trying to reach a Sasha McCandless-Connelly," the crisis management consultant responded.

There was a pause, just a half-second too long, and then the receptionist said, "I'm afraid Ms. McCandless-Connelly is out of the office on sabbatical."

Sabbatical, huh? As in, busy being sued personally? He smiled to himself. "How long will she be out?"

"Indefinitely. May I ask the nature of your call?

Perhaps another one of our attorneys can assist you."

"Oh, no—this was just a courtesy call, following up on a vendor satisfaction survey," he ad-libbed.

"I see. In that case, have a nice day."

"Thanks. You, too."

After he hung up, he stared down at the business card. The fact that she was out on leave was excellent news, evidence that his Plan B had indeed succeeded. Despite the fact that the Prescott firm insisted that Harold's complaint would be tossed out on demurrer, whatever that was, if filed, the threat of the lawsuit had served its purpose. Not only had the arbitration been postponed, but Sasha McCandless-Connelly had been sidelined entirely.

He still needed to get to the bottom of the relationship between the McCandless woman and Prachi Agarwal. He didn't care for loose ends under any circumstances. A loose end that connected a woman he'd been hired to neutralize and a woman he'd killed was one he *had* to address.

How, though? He tapped a fingernail on the business card and thought. He drew a blank. In frustration, he flicked the card off the table. It flew across the room.

A display of temper, even in private, was unwelcome.

He took a deep breath then crossed the room to fetch the business card. It had landed upside down. As he reached for it, he read the name and telephone number scrawled across the back in blue ink.

Who was Mickey Collins? And could he be the answer?

"MICKEY COLLINS."

Sasha had to smile. Leave it to Mickey to answer his own line.

"Hi Mickey. It's Sasha McCandless-Connelly," she said warmly.

"Hey, Sasha. What can I do for you?"

"I'm calling about Prachi Agarwal—you remember, the Indian scientist I referred to you last week?"

"Right. Thanks again for the referral. It looks like she's got a solid case."

"You've already met with her?"

"Sure, she came in yesterday morning."

"Yesterday?" Sasha echoed, her excitement rising.

"Yes."

"Listen, Mickey. I was supposed to see her last night, but she didn't show up."

"Okay?"

"In a sort of funny twist, I don't have her number. Could you give it to me?"

"Ahhhh," Mickey blew out a long whoosh of air. "I don't know, Sasha."

"Come on, it's just a phone number. Tell you what, I'll even buy you lunch."

"Jeez, I'm really swamped. You know how it is."

Not really, she thought. Her current schedule consisted of playing with her children, brushing the cat's fur, and taking the dog for yet another walk that he really didn't want to be on.

"We'll keep it short. I could meet you at that overpriced Italian place in the lobby of Prescott's building—right across the street from you."

"No!"

"Wow, okay." She bristled at the emotion behind his rejection.

"Sorry. I mean, uh, why don't I come to you? I have to run an errand in Shadyside anyway. I'll meet you at that Tex-Mex place on South Highland."

Realization dawned. "You don't want to be seen with me Downtown. Is that it?"

"Don't be like that. You know I don't judge. But you gotta admit, you're persona non grata in the Allegheny Bar right now. I mean, you got into a bar fight. And everybody knows that Prescott's threatened your firm with a lawsuit. It's the scuttlebutt."

She squeaked out a response, just barely. "I'm a legal pariah?"

"This too shall pass, kid. Trust me. It always blows over. I should know. But until it does, you should keep a low profile around town." His voice was kind.

But she was shaking with embarrassment and anger. She reminded herself she needed information from him. "Right, sure. Tex-Mex sounds great. What time works for you?"

"Let's do it early, before the lunch rush. I'll meet you at eleven thirty."

"See you then."

"MICKEY COLLINS," a cheerful male voice answered.

The consultant screwed up his face. What kind of lawyer answered his own telephone? He hadn't planned to speak directly to the attorney, but he switched gears seamlessly.

"Yes, good morning, Mr. Collins. This is Agent Pataki from the Department of Homeland Security."

Collins also shifted gears. His voice became cautious, distrustful. "What can I do for you, Agent Pataki?"

"I'm calling regarding a client of yours, a Dr. Agarwal."

Silence on the other end of the line. The consultant gave a grudging nod of approval. Most people rushed to fill the silence and ended up saying more than they'd planned. Not Collins; he let it hang there, untouched.

So, he continued, "It's about her visa."

"There must be some mistake. I'm not representing Dr. Agarwal on any visa or immigration issues."

Ah, but he hadn't said she wasn't a client.

The consultant probed. "She gave your name. Perhaps you're representing her on another matter and she was hoping you could handle this, as well. It'll only take a few minutes to clear up. I'll stop by your office."

"I'm afraid that's not possible. I have an appointment outside the office this morning. And, with all due respect, agent, I'm not authorized to discuss anything with you."

"Mr. Collins, you should reconsider. You don't want me to have to go to the court and get a warrant, do you?" He affected the authoritative, no-nonsense voice of every customs agent he'd ever encountered.

"Actually, Agent Pataki, that's exactly what I want you to do." Mickey Collins slammed down his phone, ending the call abruptly.

The consultant stared down at the phone in his hand in amazement.

20

Sasha watched as Mickey followed the hostess through the restaurant and slid into the seat across from her.

"Thanks for coming," she said.

"Sure thing." He gave her a bright smile as he shook out his napkin and smoothed it over his lap.

The waiter approached to take their drink order. Mickey ordered a draft beer. Sasha decided she was in a margarita mood.

"What's good here?" Mickey asked her, flipping through the menu, as the waiter left to get their drinks.

"Everything."

"You sure?" He looked around skeptically.

"Don't be fooled by all the dancing skeletons and the corny menu names. The food's solid."

She should know. She'd been eating at Mad Mex since high school, graduating from the dark and scary one near the University of Pittsburgh's campus to the well-lit, kid-friendly one in Monroeville as she aged. The fact that there was now a location within walking distance of both her home and office meant that approximately one-fourth of her body weight was margaritas and guacamole.

He nodded and closed the menu with a snap. "So, listen. You know I like you—always have. And I'm glad you sent your friend my way, but I'm not sure I can help you with whatever it is you want to know."

"I just need her telephone number. Even better, her address."

"Ah, I don't know. If she wanted you to have it, why don't you?"

"Mickey, she's missing."

That got his attention. "You said she stood you up. That's not exactly the same thing as going missing."

"She didn't just stand me up. She missed our anger management class."

He snorted. "I'm sorry, but the image of you taking a court-ordered anger management class tickles my funny bone."

"Yeah, it's a laugh riot," she said drily.

"Well, I heard you did a number on that guy in the bar. So you're pretty lucky Will was able to swing ARD for you. It's a sweet deal."

"I guess." She didn't really want to talk about her probation situation. "Can we bring this back to Prachi?"

He nodded. The waiter dropped off their drinks and a bowl of chips with house-made salsa. He took their lunch orders and disappeared into the back. Sasha watched the foot traffic outside the big wall of windows for a moment while she sipped her drink, savoring the salt that rimmed the glass.

"So, Prachi," Mickey prompted, hoisting his mug.

"Right. Did she tell you Playtime Toys threatened her with deportation?"

He nodded, piling chunky salsa onto a still-warm, blue tortilla chip. "Yeah, so?"

"So, she wouldn't miss class. It would be inviting human resources to revoke her visa— because now she's tossed from the program."

His eyes clouded. "And she knew that was the consequence?"

"Our drill sergeant—er, social worker facilitator—made it crystal clear."

"Huh. I wouldn't think she'd screw up like that. She's sharp. Real smart, great recall of the relevant facts. I mean, she's as impressive as hell. And her retaliation claim is rock solid."

"Right. And she seemed committed to fighting her company on the underlying safety issue. Which is why there's no way she skipped class of her own volition."

"Uh-oh." Mickey pushed the chips away and picked up his beer.

"Uh-oh what?"

"I got a really strange call this morning—right after you and I hung up. It was some Homeland Security agent calling about Prachi. He said she'd given him my name regarding her immigration status."

"That's not good," she breathed.

"No, it's not," he agreed. "The guy was a piece of work; he was really pumping me. Bad vibe." Mickey shook his head.

"You didn't tell him anything about her case, did you?"

"Cripes, Sasha, I've been at this since you were hanging upside down from monkey bars and getting the hang of riding a two-wheeler. Of course not. I told him to go pound salt." He looked wounded.

"Sorry. Of course you didn't. I'm just worried about her."

"You should be. If she's on ICE's radar ..." He didn't finish the thought.

"What was the guy's name?"

He gave her a strange look but answered. "He said he was Agent Pataki."

"I need a telephone number. An address. Something. Please, Mickey."

"Okay, sure, anything for you. But don't bring my name into it, okay? If she's mixed up with ICE, I want no part of it. She's at 12 Amelia. Apartment 3B."

She grinned at him. "Thanks. Can you tell me anything else? Anything you think might help me find her?"

He shook his head slowly. "What I think is you're ankle deep in doo-doo. And I don't want to put on my waders."

"What's happened to you? Where's your sense of adventure?"

He stared at her for a long time. She couldn't read his expression, but she imagined he was remembering the time they'd worked together to bend the rules of ethics almost to their breaking point in order to expose a murderer.

He drained his glass before he answered. "I'm getting too old for adventure, kid. So are you."

21

Naya was sitting on the porch swing, swaying gently back and forth, when Sasha walked up the stairs to her porch.

"Oh, hey," Sasha said in surprise. "Did Connelly toss you out?"

She laughed. "I think Flyboy and the twins must be out and about. Nobody answered the doorbell."

"How long have you been sitting here?"

"Not long." Naya took in her sheath dress and cardigan—her usual office garb. "Where were you?"

"I met Mickey Collins for lunch."

"Mickey? You're not interviewing for a job are you?"

"Bite your tongue. Do you want to come in and tell me what's going on?" Sasha asked over her shoulder as she inserted her key into the lock.

"Actually, I have to get back to the office, but I need to tell you something first." Naya patted the seat beside her.

Sasha removed the key and joined her on the porch swing. "Aren't you supposed to be out in Stowe Township getting a witness statement?"

Naya cocked her head as if to say, 'how did you know that?'

"I talked to Will this morning."

Naya looked as though she wanted to ask for details, but she returned to her own story. "Right. I'm chasing down statements for your case."

"My case?" It took her a moment to realize that Naya wasn't talking about one of the matters on Sasha's caseload but, rather, the emotional distress cause of action Steve Harold was threatening to file against her. "Was it one of the women from the bar?"

"No. The three women he was hassling are on my list for tomorrow. And then the bunch of guys who stood around and did nothing. Today, I met with Mr. Harold's ex-wife Gina."

"He's divorced? Color me shocked."

Naya laughed knowingly. "The former Mrs. Harold has an interesting story to tell."

"Let me guess. Her husband had a temper?"

"I'm sure he did, but that's not what we talked about. And I should preface this by saying I haven't had a chance to tell Will any of this yet, but I think it's a game changer as far as your defense is concerned."

A game changer? Sasha found herself leaning in, eager with anticipation. "Tell me already."

"Get this. Steve Harold is—or was, I guess—a professional stuntman."

"A stuntman? Like in the movies?"

"Exactly. He had parts in all the big movies that were filmed in the 'Burgh, right up until *The Dark Knight Rises*. That was his last role."

"What happened?"

"He figured out fraud paid better."

"What sort of fraud?"

"According to the missus, he was approached by some unsavory characters, who wanted to hire him for a series of insurance scams. He was in a bunch of car accidents that were set-ups, did some slip and falls in big-chain grocery stores. The next thing Gina knew, he'd paid off their mortgage with cash and bought a Camaro."

"Crime pays, huh?"

"It came at a cost—a few broken ribs, some sprains and fractures. But she said he was raking it in at lightning speed and spending it just as fast."

"Are you suggesting someone paid him to get into a fight with me? That the entire thing— harassing the girls, coming at me with the bottle— it was all a set up to get me arrested?"

Naya shrugged. "Gina didn't know anything about it. She said it didn't sound like the sort of game the mob guys he worked for would run. But she also said that, based on the way it went down, she was pretty sure he could have controlled the scene to make it happen."

Sasha fell silent. She was trying to remember if he'd made a genuine effort to evade the blow that broke his nose. It was impossible to say; she couldn't accurately judge the combat skills of someone she'd faced off against only once. "Maybe," she mused. "If you're telling me he was trained to take falls, he'd have to be limber and flexible enough that he should've been able to dodge me."

"Right. So why didn't he?"

"You think he let me break his nose?"

"Maybe."

"Why? So he could sue me? If so, the joke's on him. Even Prescott & Talbott has to know that claim is weaker than weak."

"Unless prevailing in court isn't his true goal," Naya countered.

"Listen, can you stop with all the Sphinx-like riddles and hints? Why else would he sue me?"

Naya gave her a look. "What else has he gotten out of it?"

"Well I'm off the arbitration. And I'm on leave."

"Mmm-hmm."

Sasha stared at her for a moment. "Sonofa ..."

"You can say that again."

She thought some more. "How? He'd have to have known I was going to be at that bar. *I* didn't even know I was going to be there until I called Maisy. It was a spur-of-the-moment plan we cooked up after I sent out the position statement early."

"Who picked the place—you or her?"

"Um ... I did. Caroline had been talking about it; she'd gone there over the weekend with her husband. I suggested it to Maisy, and she said sure, it was one of her favorite spots."

"Were you in your office when you called her?"

Sasha answered slowly, remembering. "No. I was at Jake's waiting for my coffee. They were backed up, so after I put in my order, I called Maisy to see if she was free."

"So there were people around?"

She closed her eyes and pictured the scene. "Well, sure. Mostly regulars. A couple randoms in suits." Her eyes snapped open. "Nobody who looked like Steve Harold."

"But anybody in there could have been working with Harold, just hanging out waiting for you. I mean, you do stop in for an afternoon coffee every day."

"Still ... it's farfetched."

"It is. But that doesn't make it impossible. We both ought to know that one by now," Naya said.

True enough.

"Speaking of farfetched stories, try this on for size. The reason I stopped by this morning was to tell you and Will that one of the women in my anger management class just happens to work at Playtime Toys."

Naya's right eyebrow shot up to her hairline.

"You think that's a coincidence?"

"Sort of? Maybe? It's not as though she pumped me for information or anything. In fact, she didn't even mention that she worked there. She told me she was there on a trumped-up disciplinary charge from work. She said she uncovered some safety issue. She took it to management and they shrugged it off. Suddenly, she was on probation and taking a mandatory anger management class."

"Harsh."

"Right? She wasn't willing to let it go. She didn't tell me any details, but whatever was wrong, it showed up on some test. Doesn't that sound like it's a product issue?"

Naya shrugged. "Maybe. They have to test for all kinds of things—lead, phthalates, that little parts won't come off and block kids' windpipes. It could be one of a dozen things."

"Anyway, this woman told me she would redo the test if they didn't. Then she doesn't show up again. It's weird."

"You know, even though you're on leave, you probably shouldn't be talking to her about this stuff. I mean, we do have an active case against her employer. Conflicted, much?"

Sasha shook her head. "She never told me where she worked or any details about the safety problem. She was mostly just venting about being railroaded. I hooked her up with Mickey Collins, because it sounded like she might have a retaliation claim."

"Sounds like it," Naya agreed. "How'd you find out she works at Playtime Toys?"

"I started poking around when she didn't show up for class."

She didn't have to say more. She and Naya shared a well-developed love for snooping.

"Holy moly. What did Will say?"

She sighed. "Will said you guys can't tell Recreation Group about any of this because it's all speculation. He thinks Prachi Agarwal has to be the one to come forward with it."

Naya gave her a knowing look. "So you're trying to track her down. You need some help?"

Sasha wrinkled her nose. "I think I can work on that angle. What I really need help with is finding out which product it is. Little kids could be in danger, Naya."

"Or not. You don't know that."

"Help prove me wrong then."

"Uh-uh. No way."

"Just give me a list of products that are subject to consumer product safety testing. I'm sure it's one of the schedules to one of the documents they produced during due diligence."

"Mac, no. You know, this could all be part of the set up. This woman feeds you misinformation; you take it to our client; they bring it up in the arbitration; Playtime Toys proves it's false; and the firm gets smacked with some sort of malpractice or misconduct suit."

The thought had crossed her mind. But Prachi had never even mentioned Playtime Toys.

"Naya, please. I know this deal is important to you, but—"

She shook her head. "That's not it, and you know it. I'm sorry, but no. You need to keep your nose clean. Leave it alone."

"Or what? I'm on criminal probation and I've been ousted from the law firm I created. I don't have much left to lose."

Naya pursed her lips. "But I do." She stood up and walked away, down the stairs to the sidewalk, without looking back.

Sasha swayed back and forth on the swing and watched her go.

22

The consultant walked through the entrance to the bar and sized up the crowd. It was a hard-drinking local joint on the South Side. Not one of those shiny tourist spots on Carson Street aimed at sports fans and college students. This was a neighborhood dive, hidden back on a narrow, crooked side street, sitting diagonally from an all-night Laundromat and next to a sad-looking corner store. The place stank of stale beer and cigarettes, and the rows of drinkers—almost all men, almost all white—didn't look up when the door opened and light spilled into the dim interior. He was glad he'd had the foresight to wear jeans and a T-shirt because one of his bespoke suits would've stood out in a bad way.

He shouldered his way through the crowd until he found Steve Harold nursing a beer at a scarred wooden table. He dropped into the seat across from the man. "What's so urgent?"

Harold took a pull of his beer and wiped the foam from his mouth before answering. "I need an escape plan. You gotta get me out of this court case. Pronto."

The consultant frowned. "I don't 'gotta' do anything. I suggest you remember to whom you're speaking."

Harold gulped nervously and wiped his hands on his faded jeans. "Right, sure. Sorry. You hired me to do a job, and I did it. I baited your woman lawyer into getting physical and I let her clean my clock." He rubbed the angry, red bump on the bridge of his nose as if remembering the strike he'd taken.

"That's right; you did. And you collected a handsome sum for your work. I then offered—and you accepted—a supplemental fee to serve as the named plaintiff in a lawsuit. I don't understand the issue, Mr. Harold. This is some of the easiest work you'll ever do. There's no danger; no risk of broken bones or internal bleeding; you're not outside in the weather. All you have to do is sit at a table and answer some questions. Not to mention, you're being represented, on my dime, by some of the finest lawyers in the city." He finished his lecture, leaned back, crossed his arms, and eyed his laborer.

"No, man, you don't understand. Her lawyer went and talked to my old lady."

"Your wife?"

"My ex, Gina. I'm still tight with the landlord—I pay her rent and all. Lefty said she had some black lady at her house yesterday. He asked her about it, and she said she was the lawyer for some chick who kicked my ass." He frowned.

The consultant didn't want to focus on his emasculation, so he moved along. "Okay, that's to be expected in litigation."

"You don't understand. Gina, she's bitter. She'll say things that might—"

"Is she aware of our arrangement?" The consultant's mind clicked as he began the cold calculations. Was he going to have to get rid of Steve Harold's ex-wife as well as the doctor? If this kept up, Dutch was going to have to name his next boat in his honor.

"No, no, nothing like that. We're not on good terms, I don't talk to her unless I have to. I don't tell anybody about my work," Harold hurried to reassure him.

"Then what's the problem?"

"We were together when I started my side hustles. She knows I've worked with some, uh, characters."

"Are you telling me your ex would have told the McCandless woman's lawyer about your insurance fraud work for the Giavone family?"

"Yeah, that's what I'm telling you. I mean, I think she would've. She's a snake."

"That is less than ideal," the consultant agreed.

"Right, we gotta pull the plug on this lawsuit—fast. Your fancy suits downtown say this claim doesn't have any teeth, anyway ... uh, sir." He hurried to add the honorific lest he get in trouble for being disrespectful.

The consultant appreciated the effort. In addition, his assessment was true. The case was weak, but it had done its job and had gotten her out of the firm. The arbitration had been delayed. All that remained was figuring out her connection to

Prachi Agarwal. And the lawsuit wasn't going to help in that regard.

"Sir?" Harold asked tentatively, jerking him back to the present.

"I'm thinking."

"Oh, sorry." Harold jumped at his sharp tone.

The consultant exhaled through his nose. A display of anger was a display of weakness, he reminded himself. He waited until he could speak in a perfectly calm, neutral voice. Then he said, "I understand your concern, Mr. Harold. I agree that we'll have to change course. I just hope it's not too late."

Relief washed over Harold's craggy face. Then a new worry bloomed in his eyes. "Are you gonna want your money back?" he asked haltingly.

As if that money weren't already long gone. "No. Keep it. In return, I'll expect your continued silence."

"Totally. I won't say a thing. Can I buy you drink?" Steve Harold gestured toward the bar.

"No. I'm leaving. But your next one's on me. I appreciate your honesty." He clasped Harold's shoulder. Then he tossed a twenty-dollar bill on the table.

He pushed his way out of the musty bar and

stood on the street, taking in a long breath of the fresh, evening air. This assignment was starting to be more trouble than it was worth. And all the trouble seemed to lead back to a single source: Sasha McCandless-Connelly.

23

Sasha laced up her running shoes and pulled her hair back into a low ponytail.

"I'm going for a run," she called toward the kitchen, where Connelly and the twins were baking banana bread for breakfast.

"Have fun," he called back. The twins were too busy measuring flour and smashing bananas to even look up.

She jogged out the door and down the stairs. It was one hundred percent true that she was going for a run. It also just so happened that the path she'd mapped out would take her past Prachi Agarwal's address in Bloomfield, less than a mile and a half from her own home.

As she ran toward Liberty Avenue, she raised

her face to the early-morning sun and let the light wash over her. It was early enough that if Prachi wasn't missing, Sasha'd be liable to catch her before she left for work. But she had little expectation that she'd find her at home. She was gone. Sasha could just *feel* it.

Stop that. You sound demented, she told herself.

She maintained a steady pace until she reached Amelia Street. Then she slowed to a jog and rehearsed her cover story to account for how she happened to be in Prachi's apartment building.

As she pounded up the stairs to the third floor, she acknowledged to herself that her fabricated story was sort of thin. Okay, terribly thin. It probably didn't much matter though. In the unlikely event Prachi was there, Sasha imagined she'd be glad to see a friendly face.

What if Naya's right, though, and Prachi's in on it?

She batted that worry away and paused in front of Apartment 3B to catch her breath. Then gave a gentle knock at the door. She strained to listen closely but heard no activity on the other side.

She waited a moment, and then she knocked again, louder this time.

"Prachi?" she called softly. "Dr. Agarwal, it's me, Sasha, from anger management."

Nothing.

More out of reflex than out of hope, she tried the doorknob. To her considerable amazement, it turned in her hand—unlocked.

She resisted the urge to thank her good fortune and barrel inside. Instead, she stood outside the door and considered the various reasons why Prachi's door might not be locked—most of them bad.

Accordingly, when she did creep across the threshold, she did so on full alert, scanning the apartment for an ambush or worse. The air was still and quiet, and a quick canvas of the small space confirmed it was empty. She closed and locked the door behind her—she saw no reason to let any other would-be visitors take her by surprise.

Then she clasped her hands together behind her back as though she were in an art museum and inspected the visible areas of the apartment inch by inch. Touching the doorknob and lock had been unavoidable, but beyond that she planned to limit her search to what was in plain sight. Now that her fingerprints were in the county's criminal database, it would behoove her to be cautious.

The apartment was sparkling clean and spare,

which seem to fit what little she knew about its occupant's personality. The kitchen counters gleamed; no dishes sat in the drying rack; everything was in its place. The tea kettle resting on the stove struck a slightly discordant note; it was badly dented, the metal crushed in as though it had taken a bad tumble at some point. She turned in a slow circle. The only other item that seemed out of place in the kitchen was a bound journal that sat open on the small oak table against the wall.

She walked over to it and peered down at the page. Her heart skipped as she read the words, once and then again, trying to assign them some meaning other than the most obvious. Her hands shook as she took her iPhone from the armband she used while running.

She pulled up her camera app and leaned over to snap a picture of the note.

Then she did one more circuit through Prachi's entire space: hallway; bedroom; bathroom; small living area; and back to the kitchen. Nothing else caught her eye. In light of the note, she wished more than ever that she could open drawers, cabinets, and closets. But she restrained herself. Even though she could craft a reasonable story about having become friendly with Prachi that would explain away her prints if the issue ever arose, the story would be perjurious. And she didn't need to compound her crimes.

So she gave the apartment a final backward glance, unlocked the door, and let herself out, using the hem of her tank top to wipe down the doorknob and lock.

Although she'd run at a decent pace on her way to Prachi's, she ran home even faster—at a virtual sprint—fueled by anxiety at what she'd seen and worry over what to do next.

The twins worked together building either a castle or a train yard or possibly a castle/train yard. Mocha slept curled up on the hearth. Java stretched out on the back of the couch. Leo tried to enjoy the after-dinner domestic bliss, but his wife's incessant squirming beside him proved to be a distraction. He glanced over at her, but her eyes were still fixed on her book.

She hadn't turned the page in several minutes, though, so he felt sure he wasn't disturbing her reading when he leaned over and said, "What's wrong?"

She lifted her head. "Nothing's wrong."

"Sasha—"

She tilted her head toward the twins as if to say, *'We can talk about this later, when they're asleep.'*

"They aren't paying the slightest bit of attention to us. Talk to me."

She marked her page and closed the book. Then she twisted her body toward his on the couch. "Okay, don't be mad," she began with a small sigh.

He wondered why it was that when his wife started a story that way it never ended with 'I went a little crazy at an end-of-season sale' or 'I committed us to dinner with my family without checking with you first.' No, in Sasha McCandless-Connelly's world, 'don't be mad' invariably preceded some tale of impending doom, murder, or mayhem. But then, that was part of her quirky charm.

"I won't be mad," he promised as he steeled himself for whatever news was to come.

She rewarded him with a tiny smile. "Thanks. So, you know how I had lunch with Mickey Collins yesterday?"

"Sure. Although we didn't really get a chance to talk afterward—how'd it go?"

"Aside from the fact that he was reluctant to be seen in public with me because my reputation precedes me in the Pittsburgh legal community, it was fine."

Ouch. Although she didn't say much, he knew she was struggling with her current status. As long as he'd known her—and for years before they'd met —she'd been the golden girl, the rising star. It had to be tough for her to accept that people were looking askance at her. "I'm sorry, babe." He patted her arm.

"Thanks. I know there's nothing I can do about it now. But eventually the truth will come out."

Something about the way she said it made him pause. "What truth is that?"

"I don't know yet. But I'm pretty sure I'm caught up in something I don't fully understand."

"You think this because of your lunch with Mickey?"

"Yes. And a visit from Naya. And something that happened on my run this morning."

He leaned back, stretched his arm along the back of the couch, earning a baleful look from the cat, and said, "Why don't you tell me what's going on?"

She cut her eyes over to the twins. He followed her gaze. They were still fully occupied by their architectural wonder. She blew out a breath.

"Okay, let me start at the beginning. Mickey said Prachi Agarwal came into his office for a case evaluation on Monday morning. He told her she had a solid claim, and she left in a good mood. He hasn't heard from her since then, and she didn't mention leaving town. But then she missed anger management class."

"Right. I'm with you so far."

"Mickey also said he got a weird phone call yesterday, right after I called him about meeting for lunch. Some man called and started asking questions about his representation of Prachi Agarwal."

Leo frowned. "Someone from her office, maybe? Trying to get out in front of a retaliation claim."

She shook her head no. "The man identified himself as an Agent Pataki from Homeland Security."

He searched his memory bank but came up blank. "Never heard of the guy, but that doesn't mean anything. The Department of Homeland Security is a big umbrella; there must be a thousand agents that fall under it in some capacity—probably more."

"I figured. He told Mickey he worked with immigration."

"ICE?"

"Mickey said he didn't mention Immigration and Customs Enforcement or Customs and Border Patrol. He just generally waved his hand at immigration. And he really pressed Mickey about Prachi in a way that made alarm bells ring. Mickey told him to get a warrant and hung up on the guy. But the idea that somebody's poking around looking for Prachi doesn't sit well with me.

"Me neither," he agreed.

"But there's more. Mickey gave me Prachi's home address in case I wanted to check on her."

"Uh-oh. Did you?"

She shot him a look. "I would have stopped by yesterday, but when I got home from lunch you guys were at music and movement class, and Naya was sitting on the front porch waiting for me."

"And what did Naya have to say?"

"She spent her morning interviewing Steve Harold's ex-wife—in case Prescott does file its BS complaint against me, she and Will are preparing a defense."

"And?"

"And the former Mrs. Harold didn't have

anything nice to say about her ex. One of the things she told Naya stood out, though. He is—or was—a professional stuntman."

Leo pursed his lips. "So presumably he knows how to take a punch—or avoid one."

"We had the same thought," she said approvingly. "But his ex-wife also said he stopped doing stunts in movies and television because he found an industry that paid better. Turns out, crime does pay."

He shook his head. "You lost me," he admitted.

"Criminal fraud scams. Insurance fraud, mainly. You know the thing where one car cuts off a target car on the highway and causes the driver to hit its partner car? Steve Harold would be in the car that got hit and would end up with whiplash or a broken wrist or whatever. He also did some slip and falls in grocery stores and department stores. That sort of thing."

"This sounds like a fairly low-level criminal enterprise," he observed.

"I know. Naya said his ex-wife called him more of a freelancer. He did work for various mob families or gangs, but he basically worked for the highest bidder. I'm not saying he's a criminal mastermind, but it sounds like he's for hire to anybody with a big enough bank account."

He still wasn't entirely sure where she was going with this. "Do you think somebody hired him to get into a fight with you?"

She gave a little shrug. "Maybe. It's not unthinkable."

"It's pretty far-fetched. Think of all the moving parts involved. He'd have to know you were going to be at the bar. He'd have to know that there would be women there he could harass. He'd have to know that you would play Good Samaritan."

"Naya and I talked about this. I called Maisy and suggested we meet at that bar. I called from Jake's while I was waiting for my coffee. Anybody could have heard me."

"You think somebody was hanging out in Jake's just hoping to eavesdrop?"

"I think it's possible. I do stop in every afternoon. The rest would be easy. That bar is a hot spot—there was pretty much guaranteed to be *somebody* there he could hit on who wouldn't appreciate it."

"And anybody who knows anything about you —or has access to Google—would know you'd step in."

She made a sheepish face. "Probably."

"But that means Playtime Toys had Steve Harold waiting in reserve."

"Right."

"And that seems like a lot of trouble to go through to—what, get a postponement of the arbitration hearing?"

"Which is why I think I'm caught up in something bigger. And so is Prachi Agarwal."

He studied her drawn, tense face. "What happened during your run?"

"So I happened to run past her apartment building—"

"Oh, come on."

"Fine. I deliberately planned my route to go to her apartment."

"Was she home?"

"No. But her front door was unlocked ..."

He briefly closed his eyes. He opened them and gave his wife a look. "Listen, Sasha—"

"I know it's trespassing. But I consider her a friend, sort of. And I'm worried about her. So I just went inside to check on her."

"Tell me you didn't touch anything."

She drew herself up. "Jeez, Connelly, I'm not an idiot. I didn't open any drawers or closets or go through her stuff. I did touch the doorknob, obviously, but I wiped it down with my shirt."

"It's better than nothing," he mumbled. "So did you find anything?"

"The big thing I found was that her house was completely clean."

"Well, she's single and has no kids," he said, looking around their living room which was a jumble of toys, baskets of folded laundry waiting to be carried upstairs, and sections from Sunday's *The New York Times,* which now seemed to take them nearly the entire week to read. "Or pets, I'll bet," he added, just as a tumbleweed of Java/Mocha fur drifted gently along the hallway, skimming the hardwood floor.

"Sure, but this goes beyond single-living-alone-woman clean. Think more like sparkling. Spotless."

"Some people have that personality. A scientist/computer genius would seem to be a likely candidate for fastidiousness."

"I suppose. Because everything was so clean and orderly, the one thing that *was* out of order really stood out." She took out her phone and pulled up the picture she'd taken of the note. She handed it to Leo.

He squinted at the image, reading what could only be fairly described as a suicide note. His heart thudded in his chest. He read it again. "This is bad."

"It's not good," she agreed. "I don't want to read too much into it, but ..."

He rested the phone on the arm of the couch and enveloped her hands in his. "I think you need to prepare yourself now for the fact that she's probably, you know, gone."

She nodded, but he could see in her eyes that she wasn't convinced. "Unless you know something I don't," he added.

"No, but I just wonder if maybe Agent Pataki or some other immigration enforcement agent showed up and she got spooked and bolted. You *could* maybe read the note that way."

"Maybe," he allowed. "I'll tell you what—I'll check into it tonight after the twins are asleep."

"Really? You'll do your secret agent thing?"

He nodded. "Yes."

"In that case, you can do it while I get them ready for bed." She popped to her feet.

"Are you sure? It's my night."

"Positive."

"You've got a deal," he told her. Tapping into a

secure government database without leaving a trace was approximately seven thousand times easier than getting toddler twins down for the night.

SASHA TIPTOED into the home office, feeling flush with victory. Connelly swiveled in his chair to look at her.

"Great success," she whispered triumphantly. "Now let's just hope they don't sleep like babies."

They shared a quiet laugh. Only after they'd become parents had they realized that 'sleeping like a baby' was a complete misnomer.

She perched on the edge of the desk. "Have you found anything?" she asked, struggling to keep the hope out of her voice.

He blew out a frustrated breath and dragged his fingers through his thick hair, creating a sea of tiny spikes. "I haven't found anybody named Pataki."

"So the guy lied to Mickey."

"Well he could've been lying about his identity. Or he could've been lying about his assignment. Or he could be undercover. Or he could be on loan to Homeland Security from another agency. Or he could have a role like mine and Hank's, which isn't going to be in any database."

She frowned at that. How were they going to track down the guy if he belonged to some shadow agency that didn't even officially exist?

He went on. "But who knows? All I can say about Agent Pataki is I can't say anything for sure."

"Okay, so forget Pataki. What about Prachi?"

He closed one window and enlarged another. "This is Prachi Agarwal's visa application and supporting documentation. Do you have your phone?"

She nodded and pulled it out of her back pocket.

"Pull up the picture you took of her note."

Sasha's stomach clenched at the mention of the note, but she nodded and pinched the screen to zoom in on the picture. "Got it."

"Okay. Come here and take a look at this." He pulled her onto his lap and pointed to an image of a handwritten response Prachi Agarwal had given to a series of questions about her position at Playtime Toys.

The script was straight up and down, almost vertical. It was a clean and precise, almost masculine, cursive. Even her signature was all straight lines and angles. It was not at all surprising for someone with an analytical bent who worked in science and technology, but it was all wrong.

Sasha leaned in for a closer look and then looked back at her photo. "That's not right."

Connelly nodded. "They're not a match at all."

The note was written in a stereotypically feminine hand. Flowery, flowing script with lots of curlicues and big, sweeping letters.

"So one of these is a forgery."

"Oh, this one is real. She would have written these answers in front of a Customs and Border Patrol agent." He jabbed at the monitor. "Of course you'd need a handwriting expert to say definitively, but wouldn't you say the note you found in her notebook is trying almost too hard to look like it was written by a woman? It's as though a man who didn't have a sample of Prachi's handwriting wrote this note."

"Do you think it was this Agent Pataki, if he exists?"

He shrugged. "I don't want to speculate. And I don't want to worry you more than you already are …"

"But?"

"But there's an alternative theory. It's not a great one, though."

"Just tell me, Connelly."

He turned her so she was facing him before he answered. "Some of the Customs and Border Patrol folks have, on occasion, gotten a bit too enthusiastic."

"You don't say," she said dryly. It wasn't exactly a revelation that there were rogue federal agents out in the wild. But this wasn't the time to get into a big discussion about it with Mr. Law and Order.

"Some of the detention facilities are dark sites," he persisted. "Being sent there, it's almost like rendition on U.S. soil. The detainee's name never appears on a prisoner manifest. If they're not on the list, they don't exist. They're not entitled to a speedy determination. They don't have access to counsel. They're just disappeared."

A wave of nausea rolled through her. "Do you think that's what happened to Prachi?" she asked, her voice cracking.

"I don't know. I could see an agent, maybe tipped off by Playtime Toys just to rattle her, getting carried away. And writing the note to cover it up. Or it could be something else entirely. Regardless, I guess what I'm saying is I agree with you that you and Prachi Agarwal are mixed up in something. Something that inspired someone to fake what seems to be a suicide note for a woman who's gone missing."

"We have to go back to her apartment," she murmured.

He took her in his arms. "No. We don't." He pulled her tight and spoke with his mouth close to her ear. "You're going to go to bed. Or take a bath. Meditate. Something. I'm going to call a buddy at the police department and ask them to stop by her place."

"But what if the local police stumble into an active federal investigation? Won't you be in hot water?" she asked, tilting her head up to see his face.

He worked his jaw. "One, if there's an investigation, it's so off the books that even I don't have access to it. That's unlikely. And two, that's why I'm calling in a favor. This isn't going to trace back to me. And, more importantly, it's not going to trace back to you. Okay?"

She hesitated. She hated to involve him in her mess; but, then again, what was marriage if not an agreement to share messes? So she nodded. "Okay."

25

Leo's cell phone chirped to life early Friday morning. *PBP* flashed across the screen. Pittsburgh Bureau of Police. That was quick.

"Hey," he called into the living room. "I need to step outside and take this call. There's still half a pot of coffee."

She looked up from the colorful, floor puzzle she was working on with Finn and Fiona and nodded.

He accepted the call as he walked through the kitchen and out into their small backyard. "This is Leo Connelly."

Cheryl Minet, a Zone 4 patrol officer he'd met during a joint sting operation, was all business.

"Sorry I didn't call sooner. There was a little kerfuffle over whether the address you gave me was within our boundaries or in Zone 5."

"And?"

She laughed. "There's this little finger of Zone 4 that protrudes into Zone 5's boundaries. On the zone map, it looks like we're flipping them the bird. Lucky for you, Amelia Street's in the finger."

He chuckled. "Great."

"Yeah, but I'll tell you straight up, the news isn't great. We did the welfare check first thing this morning. The Agarwal woman's apartment was unlocked and empty."

He'd expected as much. He was more interested in what else she had to say. "No evidence of where she might have gotten to?"

"So here's the thing. That apartment is totally clean. Too clean."

Exactly what Sasha had said. "You mean it's clean as in there's no evidence of foul play?"

"I mean it's clean as in there are no fingerprints anywhere. Somebody who knows what he's doing spent some time in there with bleach and enzyme removers."

Leo's pulse twitched wildly under his ear. "Are you sure?"

"Listen, I don't have the experience you have, but I've been doing this long enough to know that apartment was sanitized by a pro. There was a note in a journal on the kitchen table that we're processing now. If it weren't for the absence of fingerprints, the note would lead me to believe your Prachi Agarwal took off and went somewhere to kill herself. But dead people don't generally wipe away all traces of their own existence, you know?"

He nodded. Someone had been a bit *too* thorough. "What are your next steps?"

"I talked to my commander. We're treating it as missing person/possible foul play situation. We've got a guy doing a canvas of the neighborhood. We'll send a unit to her place of work. And we've reached out to the landlord. Boss wants to know if any federal agency is running a parallel investigation. I didn't mention your name. Should I?"

"No. As of now, we consider this a local law enforcement matter. Dr. Agarwal happens to be an acquaintance of my wife. She was worried about Prachi, so I told her I would call in a favor. Make sure my name doesn't show up anywhere in a report."

"No worries. I gotcha. This one goes in the favor bank."

"Definitely." He knew how the system worked. He now owed Officer Minet one. It might be months, or years, before she collected. But she would.

They said their goodbyes, and he ended the call. The fact that Prachi Agarwal's apartment had been wiped clean sent a shiver down his spine despite the late-morning sunshine warming the air.

He hated to involve Hank, but it was time. They weren't currently working an active investigation, which suited both of them just fine seeing as how they were pretty busy running their respective households. But he needed to bounce some ideas off his mentor and boss.

Hank answered after several rings. "What's up?"

"Do you have time to talk?"

"I have about 10 minutes before we have to leave for the orthodontist's office."

"That'll do. I'll spare you all the details, but there's a missing woman—Dr. Prachi Agarwal. She's here on an H-1B skilled worker visa."

"Define missing."

"She met with a lawyer on Monday morning about a potential employment claim. Demeanor was normal. No mention of any out-of-town travel. Nobody's seen her since. She should have been in Sasha's anger management class on Monday night, but she was a no-show."

"Anger management? Who did Dr. Agarwal punch in the nose?"

"Ha. Unlike my lovely wife, she wasn't court-ordered to attend. She's on probation at work for slamming a door or something. Her employer told her if she didn't take the class they'd revoke their sponsorship of her visa and she'd be deported."

"So we wouldn't expect her to miss class."

"Bingo. Couple other things. Somebody called her employment lawyer asking questions. He claimed to be a guy named Pataki from Homeland Security."

"Doesn't ring a bell."

"Didn't for me either. And Sasha stopped by her apartment yesterday. Nobody was home but the front door was unlocked."

Hank groaned. "Let me guess. Nancy Drew let herself in."

"Of course she did. She poked around but didn't touch anything. She said the place was squeaky clean, and there was a note on the kitchen table that could be interpreted as a suicide note."

"Interesting."

"It gets more interesting. I took a peek at Prachi Agarwal's immigration file." Leo paused to see if Hank would object to his self-help.

All Hank said was, "I trust you did it in a fashion that didn't leave any electronic fingerprints."

Leo huffed, almost as offended as Sasha had been the night before at the suggestion that she might have been sloppy. "Jeez, Hank. Of course I didn't."

"Just checking. Did you learn anything useful?"

"I'll say. The handwriting on the note in the apartment doesn't match her handwritten interview answers in the file—and I mean, it's not even close."

"So we have a missing woman, a fake suicide note, and a weird phone call that may or may not have originated from the Department of Homeland Security," Hank mused. "You should ask the local PD to send over a unit for a welfare check. See what they turn up."

"I'm a step ahead of you. I called Cheryl Minet last night. By the way, she's got one in the plus column now. Anyway, Zone 4 is opening an investigation because—get this—the place has been sanitized."

Hank gave a low whistle. "That doesn't sound like ICE or Homeland Security. If anything, it sounds like us. And we haven't disappeared her." A heavy silence followed. Then he said. "I can think of three, maybe four, teams that might clean an apartment like that. But if any of them are involved …"

"It means she's dead," Leo finished Hank's thought.

"Well, yeah, most likely. Let's keep our fingers out of this pie for now. Let the police work it. But depending on how tight Sasha was with this Dr. Agarwal, you two probably want to take precautions."

Leo exhaled loudly. "Right. I don't want to make you late for the orthodontist, so I'll just say it looks like Sasha's mixed up in whatever got this woman disappeared. It might even be tied to her bar fight."

"I'm serious about the precautions."

"I know."

"In the meantime," Hank went on, "I'll make some calls and ask some low-key questions to some of the guys at ICE, but as far as I know, they don't sanitize apartments. Although, these days, who can say for sure."

"I appreciate the help."

"Don't mention it."

Leo shut down his phone and slipped it into his pocket. Then he turned his face up and let the sun warm it for a moment before he walked back into the house.

CONNELLY CAME BACK into the living room with a heavy weight on his shoulders. Sasha could almost see him straining under the burden. She finished off the alphabet train puzzle and handed Finn and Fiona a stack of hardback Dr. Seuss books before joining Connelly near the fireplace.

"What's wrong?" she asked not much louder than a whisper.

"Pittsburgh Police checked Prachi's apartment. It's totally clean—not just of your prints. There are *no* prints."

"What do you mean, no prints? Her finger-prints have to be there." She looked at him in utter bafflement.

"You'd expect them to be, but they aren't."

"How? Why?"

He just shook his head. "It's concerning," he finally said. "Would you call Mickey Collins and find out if that Agent Pataki has contacted him again? If he has, try to get a telephone number for him, okay?"

Connelly's voice was tight with tension. She gave him a careful look. Then she nodded.

"Okay. I'll call from upstairs. So, tag you're it." She pointed to the twins and the pile of books.

She took the stairs by twos, her heart beating wildly. Connelly had a great poker face—usually. The fact that his worry was showing was enough to make her worried.

True to form, Mickey answered his own phone.

"Hi, Mickey. It's Sasha," she said as soon as she heard his voice.

"Hi. Did you catch up with Prachi?"

"No. I stopped by her place yesterday, but she wasn't there." Sasha decided to tell him the truth, just not the whole truth and nothing but the truth.

"I hope she turns up soon," he mused.

"You and me both. Listen, I was wondering if that Agent Pataki's called back or anything?"

"I didn't talk to him. Hang on a sec." She could

hear him rifling through papers on his desk, most likely a stack of message slips. "Nope," he confirmed.

"And you didn't get his number, right?"

"Right."

"Do me a favor and let me know if he reaches out to you again."

"Sure thing. Is that all you wanted? I'm not trying to give you the bum's rush, but I have a jury trial starting this afternoon, so ..."

"You should know that the police are looking into Prachi's disappearance. I think they may suspect foul play," she blurted.

"Holy cow."

"Yeah. Is there anything you want to tell me?"

"About Prachi's case? No."

She sighed. "I'll let you go. Good luck with your trial."

She ended the call and trudged back downstairs to break the news to Connelly. *Now what?*

26

Sasha had to do something other than sit around and wait for the other shoe to drop. Connelly was roaming through the house like a caged panther. He was holding something back from her, and she was pretty sure that it was his belief that Prachi Agarwal had been murdered.

She dialed Will's number. After a brief chat with Caroline, who filled her in on the office goings on, she was connected with Will.

"How're you doing?" he asked in a kind voice.

"I've been better," she said, unwilling or unable to muster the strength to lie convincingly.

"I'm sorry."

She brushed aside the concern. "I'd like to talk to you and Naya about Steve Harold's complaint."

"I take it she filled you in on her interview with his ex-wife?"

"She gave me an overview," Sasha answered, "but I want to set up a time to come in and sit down with you both."

He hesitated and then said, "I just don't think it's a great idea for you to come into the office. It would be confusing for folks if you came in while you're supposed to be out on leave."

"Come on, Will. I came in all the time when I was on maternity leave. Our people are smart enough to handle a Sasha sighting."

"I know, but this is a different situation. It's just ... cleaner this way. Why don't I have Naya step into my office and we can put you on the speaker."

"Fine."

He placed her on hold to call Naya. As she waited, her frustration began to mount, and she found herself pacing back and forth across the kitchen floor.

"Naya's on her way," Will said when he returned to the line.

After a brief silence, which Sasha made no effort to fill with chitchat, she heard Naya's voice.

"Hey, Mac."

"Hi," she responded.

"Okay, the gang's all here. Naya has a legal pad to take notes; my door's closed; we're all yours," Will said in a cheerful voice.

"So, Naya, as I told Will, I'm calling as your client with regard to Steve Harold's draft complaint," Sasha tried to ignore the weirdness she felt talking to her two closest colleagues and good friends this way. "Have you heard anything more from Prescott & Talbott?"

Will fielded the question. "No. I did reach out to Kevin Marcus yesterday afternoon. I left him a message explaining that we've begun working up the case file and we've uncovered some interesting facts. I encouraged him to rethink their complaint. So far, he hasn't responded. I'm sure he's got to huddle with whichever associate is actually doing the work on this matter first."

"I'd like to turn up the heat," Sasha said.

"How do you mean?" Naya asked.

"Knowing what we now know about Mr. Harold's history, I'd like you to draft a counterclaim."

"On what theory?"

Sasha smiled to herself. "You're the lawyers. Come up with one."

"Come on, Mac." Naya laughed.

"I don't know. Pick one—defamation; interference with contractual relationship; fraud? But this can't stand. It's impacting my reputation and the firm's financial situation."

"Well, maybe ..." Will mused. "We'll have to look at the case law."

"That's fine. I don't want to file something specious, obviously. But I also don't want to treat this Harold guy—or Prescott & Talbott, for that matter—with kid gloves. We all know the true purpose of their draft complaint is to cow me. I'm not going to be cowed. So you can tell Marcus I'm not interested in settling. Tell him if they want to file, file. And then tell him to be on the lookout for our counterclaim. But I'm not going to sit here and let their ridiculous complaint hang over me like a cloud."

Will began to hem and haw.

Naya piped up. "What if we keep our powder dry on the counterclaim and tell them we're going to seek a motion for pre-complaint discovery?"

Sasha considered that for a moment. "That's kind of brilliant. We'd end up positioning ourselves as the plaintiff, and we wouldn't have to stretch to come up with a claim that might not be solid. But we could still compel answers to interrogatories and notice Harold's deposition. What do you think, Will?"

"Well, while it's not my nature to rattle a hornet's nest, I do understand that you're impatient and frustrated. And there is merit to holding Prescott's feet to the fire. Yes, Naya's suggestion is a good compromise. I'll call Marcus again and tell him they have until close of business Monday to affirmatively state that they are not going to file or we'll move for pre-complaint discovery. The only danger is that we'll force their hand, and they'll file this afternoon rather than admit they were bluffing."

"I'm willing to risk it," Sasha said. "That complaint's so flimsy that even without evidence of Steve Harold's fraud scams it won't survive a demurrer."

"Very good," Will said. He added, "I know this is difficult for you. It's not easy for us either."

"I know." She felt shaky and emotional, as if she might start to cry. She took a breath and plowed ahead, "While I have you both on the phone, I want to ask you to reconsider going to

Recreation Group with my concerns about Play-time Toys."

"Does this mean you found Prachi Agarwal?" Will asked.

"No. She's still missing. The police did a welfare check and found a note and some other evidence at her apartment that's led them to open a criminal investigation," Sasha said in a small, tight voice.

"What kind of criminal investigation?" Naya asked.

"I don't know the details. But I think she's presumed dead."

"Dead?" Will echoed.

"Please don't say anything about that to Recreation Group. I don't know how much the people at Playtime Toys know, and I don't want it to get back to them through us. But I do think that, in light of the police investigation, we can't sit on the information she shared any longer."

"Ah, let me think about this," Will said.

"Think fast," she told him.

27

As a rule, the crisis management consultant wasn't fond of lunch meetings. And he generally sought to avoid mid-price chain restaurants—especially those that embraced a theme. But when a client sounded as close to the edge as Charles Merriman sounded, he made all sorts of exceptions. So, he settled into the pleather booth and perused the colorful vinyl menu. What in the devil was a cod burger?

He waved away the waitress, who appeared to be dressed as a pirate's wench, explaining, "I'm waiting for someone." Then he checked his watch.

When he looked up, Merriman was sliding into the booth across from him. "Dr. Agarwal's been missing for four days," he said without preamble.

"Yes, I suppose she has." The consultant sincerely hoped that little announcement wasn't why he'd been dragged to Salty Sal's Seaside Fish Shack, which was not even remotely seaside, situated as it was in a suburban strip mall. The most he could say to commend it was that it was more than twenty miles from Playtime Toys' office building, so they were unlikely to be spotted by any employees out on a lunch break.

Merriman glanced furtively around the mostly empty restaurant and leaned over the table. "Apparently someone called the police and asked them to check on her. They went to her apartment this morning. Then they showed up at the office, asking a lot of questions." His voice quavered.

"Did you mention the products she stole?"

"Of course not. I can't risk drawing attention to that issue. I did instruct our human resources director to show the police her personnel records, including the write-up and referral to anger management. I strongly suggested that she was emotionally unbalanced. But I can't have law enforcement poking around our offices. Not now. What do I do?" He was nearly wailing.

"The first thing you need to do is to pull yourself together."

"Yes, right." The man straightened his spine.

"Good. Now, I imagine that the police would have found the same note that I saw in her apartment. I'm sure they're in the process of coming to the regrettable conclusion that she's taken her own life. Of course they need to investigate. It was smart to introduce the idea that she wasn't in a good place mentally. You just need to be patient. And don't panic." He spoke in the soothing tone one would use to calm a frightened child.

The CEO exhaled. "Have you had any luck locating Dr. Agarwal?" he asked hopefully.

"No, I don't have the foggiest idea where she could be," he answered truthfully.

Merriman gasped. "I was just struck by a thought. What if the police find your fingerprints in her apartment?"

He arched his eyebrow and pinned the man with a dour look. "They won't."

The pirate wench waitress returned and they ordered a couple fish sandwiches and iced teas.

After she departed with their orders, Merriman gave him an embarrassed smile. "I feel silly dragging you out here. I just ... I suppose I panicked."

"It's understandable," the consultant assured

him. "I wouldn't expect you to know how to handle a visit from the police. Why would you?"

WHEN HE RETURNED to his hotel room after choking down his fried fish sandwich and sending Merriman on his way with some final words of encouragement, it was already mid-afternoon. He had one final call to make.

He dialed Kevin Marcus's line at Prescott & Talbott.

"Mr. Marcus's office. May I help you?"

"I need to speak to Kevin."

"And who may I say is calling?" the secretary responded in the same silky voice she'd used to answer.

"I'm calling regarding the Steve Harold matter against Sasha McCandless."

"Mr. Harold?"

"No, this isn't Mr. Harold. I'm financing the litigation. And I need to speak to Marcus. Now."

"Yes, sir. One moment, sir." The secretary morphed from officious gatekeeper into flustered assistant in a flash.

Kevin Marcus's voice boomed on the other end

of the line. "Why is my secretary on the verge of tears?"

Only one of his former fraternity brothers could get away with speaking to him that way. "Sheesh, what a delicate flower," he countered. "Listen, I need you to pull the plug on the complaint."

"What? Why?"

"Why does it matter? Just do it. Call Will Volmer and tell him your client is dropping the claim against Sasha McCandless-Connelly."

"It's not that easy," Kevin protested.

"Sure it is. It's exactly that easy."

"Wrong. And as a matter of fact, I heard from Volmer just this morning, calling your bluff. I have until close of business on Monday to file or they're going to seek pre-complaint discovery. I can't tell them now that we're not going to sue her. It'll make you look weak."

"It won't make me look any way. It might make you or Harold look weak, but that's not my problem."

He listened as Kevin sputtered wordlessly for a moment. Then the lawyer found his voice. "I'm urging you to reconsider."

"Aren't you the one who told me the claim was

a piece of crap?"

"I believe what I said was that it lacks merit and is unlikely to survive a demurrer, which is the state court equivalent of a motion to dismiss."

"Right. And that sounds like lawyer for 'it's a piece of crap.'"

Kevin laughed mirthlessly. "Be that as it may. There's no guarantee that withdrawing Harold's claim means they won't pursue claims against him. The genie's out of the bottle, so to speak. And if they are going to file a lawsuit against him, it's better to have ours teed up and ready to go. Playing offense is always easier than playing defense."

"You're mixing your sports metaphors," he noted. "Listen, Kevin, I don't actually care if they sue Steve Harold. He's judgment-proof anyway. But I'm paying the bills, and I'm instructing you to shut this down."

After a long silence, Kevin said, "As you wish. I'll let Volmer know and then close out the file. Shall I send a final invoice to your banker in the Cay Carroway?"

"Yes, thanks."

"You know, it's been years since I've seen you. You never come to the reunions. If you're ever in Pittsburgh, we should—"

"I have no plans to come to town," he said as he stared down at Pittsburgh's iconic Point State Park Fountain from his wall-sized window. He dropped his cell phone as if it were crawling with bugs and dug through his wicker basket for a skein of yarn and his needles. He'd finished the lap blanket but he needed to do something with his hands.

28

Sasha had just finished drying her hair and was twisting it into a loose up-do when the doorbell rang.

"I'll get it," Connelly called up the stairs.

A moment later she heard Jordana enter the living room and greet the kids in a flurry of laughter. They loved it when Jordana babysat. She had an innate knack for art projects, and Sasha and Connelly invariably came home to a new creation and a house that looked like a glittery glue bomb had gone off.

Sasha fastened her bracelet around her wrist, grabbed her clutch from the dresser, and trotted down the stairs.

"Hi, Jordana. Could you zip me up?" she said,

turning to Connelly as she walked into the living room.

His warm hand pressed against her bare upper back and she shivered. He slowly pulled up the zipper and kissed her lightly on the nape of her neck.

"You're all set," he murmured against her skin.

Fiona looked up, and her eyes grew wide. "Mommy, you look like a princess!" she exclaimed in an awestruck tone.

Sasha laughed. "Thanks, honey." she twirled and the white skirt of her black and white cocktail dress flared out around her knees.

"Pretty Mommy," Finn agreed, fluttering his eyelashes.

"Aw, thanks." Sasha crouched on the floor and kissed both sweet faces. "Have fun with Jordana and be really, really good."

Jordana grinned broadly. "I have this great mosaic tile project we can do. Don't worry, they're not real tiles. We'll rip up colored tissue paper and make a glue paste. It'll be awesome."

"Sounds great." Sasha was already envisioning spending an hour or so pulling little squares of sticky tissue paper off her kitchen floor.

She used the mirror over the fireplace mantle

to check her reflection while she swiped a cranberry lipstick over her lips. She gave each of the twins a final lipsticked kiss, leaving a mark on each of their faces. They giggled and pointed at each other. Sasha's mother used to leave a bright red lip print on Sasha's cheek and each of her brothers' cheeks on the rare nights her parents went out. She smiled at the memory and dropped the lipstick and her cell phone into her small purse.

"Do you have any questions before we go?" she asked Jordana, her hand already on the doorknob.

"Nope. Mr. Connelly filled me in. I'll make sure Mocha gets to go out in the yard and Java gets his ear drops. The kids and I will be fine. You guys have fun." She gave them a big smile.

Connelly kissed the tops of the twins' heads then held the door open for Sasha.

"It's a nice night. Why don't we walk over to Chris and Daniel's?" he asked.

"Definitely," she said. She linked her arm through his as they strolled down their front stairs to the sidewalk.

After they'd walked about a half a block, she said, "Hey, did your police officer friend happen to say whether they found anything weird at Prachi's house?"

"She didn't mention anything, but if there was anything out of place, they'd have found it. But if they swept the apartment, they would have done a thorough job—inside the toilet tank, the duct-work, every imaginable space. Why? What are you thinking?"

"I'm thinking that she would have hid whatever it was she wanted to retest at home."

"Why?"

"Because she was on thin ice at work and she knew it. Better to sneak the thing out than have someone find it in her desk. Can you just call and ask Officer Minet if they found any toys or anything?"

"You're a lousy date," he informed her. But he pulled his cell phone from his pocket and placed the call.

She listened while he was connected to the officer and asked the question. She could hear the officer's peal of surprised laughter through the phone. She waited impatiently while Connelly yapped at the woman.

Finally, he ended the call and turned to her. "Well, you were right. They found three packages of kids' bathtub crayons in the oven, which they thought was odd since Prachi Agarwal is childless and has no bathtub, just a glass block shower stall. And also because they were in the oven."

"The oven is a classic storage spot for people who don't cook. It's just a big, empty rack," she informed him. "File it away for future reference."

"If you say so."

"What will they do with the crayons? Will they keep them as evidence?"

"Sure."

"Chain of custody, the whole deal?"

"Well, yeah. Why?"

"Because I might need them."

He looked at her for a moment with one of his typical unreadable Connelly expressions. Then he said, "Oh, there's been one other development. Officer Minet said she was just getting ready to call me. The canvas turned up a resident who was on his way back into the building after walking his dog at lunchtime the day Prachi disappeared. He ran into a white guy leaving the building. The guy with the dog said this guy seemed out of place."

"Since when is a white guy out of place in Bloomfield?" she wanted to know.

"This white guy was. His suit was a little too expensive; he looked a bit too corporate. He was just off enough that the dog walker noticed him."

"So now what?"

"They've got the resident working with a sketch artist. The police have a lead. You found out about the crayons. *Now* can we enjoy our date night?" He stuck the phone in his pocket and interlocked his fingers through hers.

"Not yet. I have a call to make."

He sighed while she dialed Mickey Collins's cell phone number. When he answered, she could tell he was at a bar or restaurant, someplace noisy, with loud conversation and louder music.

"What's up, Sasha?" he shouted.

"I don't want to interrupt your post-trial celebration," she told him. "I just have one question."

"Shoot."

"The product Prachi Agarwal was worried about—was it crayons? The police found crayons in her apartment."

Mickey paused. "Are you asking me why Prachi Agarwal had three packages of children's bathtub crayons in her oven?"

Sasha blinked. "What?"

"You know who I ran into the other day? Judge Cook. He said to tell you he said hi."

What? How drunk was he? "Mickey—"

"Good luck, kid."

Mickey ended the call. She thought for a moment. Mickey had obviously known all about the crayons. And he'd mentioned Judge Cook— the federal court judge who'd presided over the case where she and Mickey had held hands and jumped off the ethics bridge to prevent a crime. A shiver of excitement ran through her. He was confirming, without confirming, that the bathtub crayons were the product that Prachi was worried about. She was finally making some progress.

Connelly was watching her. She bumped her hip into him playfully.

"*Now,* we can enjoy our date night," she told him.

SASHA WAS LISTENING to Bertie Steinfeld, Daniel's mother and Chris's mother-in-law, describe the cruise from which she and her husband Larry had just returned. Sasha's own personal experience with cruising hadn't left her a fan, to put it mildly. But Bertie was beyond ecstatic, rapturous even.

"Then there was this intricate ice sculpture in the atrium," she was saying, making big sweeping arcs with her arms as she described the piece, when Maisy came rushing over.

"Oh thank goodness! I need you to save me," Maisy breathed.

"Save you from what?" Bertie wanted to know.

"It's a who, not a what." Maisy jerked her head. "See the guy in the blue shirt looking this way?"

Sasha stood on her tiptoes and scanned the room but all she could see was a wall of chests and shoulders. Daniel and Chris must have inordinately tall friends, she mused.

Bertie squinted into the crowd. "The man with the light brown hair and the glasses? That's Drew, he's Chris's piano tuner. He's a sweetheart—and available."

"No offense, Mrs. Steinfeld, but I'm not in the market for sweet. I'm looking for tall, dark, and dangerous."

Bertie laughed. "It sounds like you're describing Leo."

Maisy rolled her blue eyes. "Make that tall, dark, dangerous and not saddled with toddler twins."

"Good thing. He's taken. Depending on the day, the twins might be available, though," Sasha snarked.

Bertie laughed so hard she almost lost her cocktail. She tightened her grip and peered into her glass. "It looks like I need to freshen up my drink. Make sure you girls try the cookies. Daniel always hires a caterer, but I snuck some of my cinnamon drop cookies onto the trays."

"Nice talking to you, Bertie," Sasha said to the woman's back as she made her way to the bar.

Maisy turned to her and said, "You know I was just joking, right? I love spending time with Finn and Fiona—just as long as I can give them back to you at the end of the day."

"I know."

Maisy studied Sasha's face. "How you doing? I mean, really?"

"I take it you heard I'm on leave."

"Leo mentioned it while I was trying to ambush the caterer who had the shrimp tray. He almost distracted me from my mission. *Almost.*"

Sasha smiled. "I'm fine. I don't love being side-lined, obviously, but it's nice to spend time with Connelly and the kids."

"You work too hard, anyway. Treat it like a vacation—unwind, relax."

"Mmm-hmm." A vacation spent skulking into a missing woman's apartment and delving into the dirty past of a stuntman/con artist while trying to unravel a product safety issue. It was just like a spa weekend. Then a thought struck her. "Hey, wait, when's your product safety exposé going to air?"

"Next week. I'm really jazzed about it. I think investigative journalism might be it for me—I liked learning something new. Especially something that could really help people."

She hadn't seen Maisy this excited about her work in years—not since she got promoted from weekend weather girl to full-fledged reporter. "Awesome. Hey, let me ask you a question—did you learn anything about the testing of children's products?"

Maisy pursed her mouth and thought. "A little bit. Under the CPSIA, most children's toys are tested by a certified testing company for heavy metals—they're looking for a bunch of different metals, but lead's the big one. Plastic products are tested for phthalates."

"Would something like bathtub crayons fall under the heavy metals testing requirement?" Sasha asked.

"What the devil are bathtub crayons?" Maisy countered.

Sasha sipped her gin and tonic then said,

"They're pretty much what it sounds like—crayons that little kids use in the bathtub."

Maisy shook her head. "You mean to scribble on the walls and the surface of the tub? That seems like a bad idea. Next thing you know they're drawing on your living room walls with a marker and getting in trouble."

Sasha laughed. She'd always thought the same thing. "You won't believe this, but they also make markers for drawing on your windows."

"Jeez. I must be missing something. Well, anyway, if these bathtub crayons are marketed as a children's toy, then, yes, they'd have to undergo the testing."

"And if they failed?"

Maisy blew out a breath. "Companies do all sorts of gymnastics to avoid that. Re-testing gets expensive."

"How expensive can it be?"

"Well, if the product passes, sure, it's no big deal. The price of the testing is a cost of doing business—it's baked into the COGS—er, cost of goods sold. But if testing results show that there's too much of even one of those heavy metals, then you're up the creek without a paddle, as my grand-daddy would say."

"But we're talking about kids," Sasha protested.

"I know, but these guys are all about the bottom line. And once a product has failed a test, I think they're supposed to enter the information online into this publicly available, searchable complaint database. So, say you're selling wooden blocks and they test positive for unsafe levels of arsenic."

An image of Finn chewing his way through a set of antiqued, vintage alphabet blocks as if he were a beaver flashed in Sasha's mind. "Okay."

"All the other levels are good, but arsenic is slightly out of whack. You have to enter that into the database, re-run the tests, and hope the results come back clean. Otherwise, you have to announce a recall. But either way, the information is out there. And the first time little Devon or Ryan has a seizure, his frantic parents are going to scour the internet and see that bad result. Now, you're being sued."

"If the parents can't prove a connection, they won't prevail."

"Sure. But, newsflash, Sasha, lawyers aren't cheap. It'll cost money, lots of it, to defend. The cheaper route is to bury the bad test result and re-route the shipment of blocks to Mexico or Thailand."

"You're not serious."

"Happens all the time. Of course, the wrinkle is the world is global now. When I was working on my piece, I came across a company that had a huge shipment of baby chairs that failed the choking hazard test. Some little clip that looked like a round cracker would come off in the baby's mouth, slide down the windpipe, get stuck, and boom. The company diverted them to some country overseas, but the buyer was a reseller, who turned around and sold them to thrift shops and consignment shops throughout the western United States. There's was no active recall, so thousands of them were sold. There are babies all throughout Oregon, California, and Washington state choking on these baby chair clips that should never have been sold in the first place."

"That's reprehensible," Sasha breathed.

Maisy was about to answer, but the piano tuner spotted her and darted toward them. Maisy melted into the crowd.

29

Crocheting wasn't helping and knitting wasn't helping. Nothing was distracting him from the lawyer and her link to Prachi Agarwal. Sasha McCandless-Connelly was like a grain of sand in his eye or a splinter in his finger. He dropped the needles and yarn and picked up his cell phone.

"Yes?" the CEO answered cautiously, alert despite the late hour.

"You mentioned that the scientist was going to an anger management program," the consultant said, skipping the pleasantries.

"Yes. For female offenders. Human resources found a program near her home. Why?"

"No reason." He ended the call and stroked his chin.

Prachi Agarwal's apartment was less than a mile from McCandless & Volmer's office. Could they possibly have been in the same anger management program? Was that the connection? Perhaps. He would have to try to find out in the morning. Now, though, he should sleep.

He lay in bed, restless and irritated. He alternated between staring at the ceiling and clicking on the bedside lamp and staring at the business card he'd taken from Prachi Agarwal's pocket. He had to determine how the two women were connected or he'd never have peace.

He slipped back out of bed and stood at the window, looking down at the city lights and the handful of cars zipping across the bridge in the middle of the night. He wondered idly where the drivers were going to or coming from at this hour.

If he were one of his own clients—beset by anxiety and helplessness—he would tell himself to take control of the situation. So that's what he would have to do. He would find out if they were in the same anger management program and either satisfy himself that any relationship between Sasha McCandless-Connelly and Prachi Agarwal was incidental, harmless, and not a danger to him or he would simply remove the lawyer from the equation. Problem solved.

His blood pressure dropped. His pulse slowed. And his mind stopped racing in a circle. He yawned, stretched, drew the curtains, and returned to his bed. He was asleep as soon as his head hit the pillow.

IT WAS NEARLY MIDNIGHT, and the party was still in full swing when Sasha and Connelly made their escape.

From within a flurry of goodbye hugs and kisses, Daniel pulled Sasha aside and searched her face. "You and I didn't really get to talk tonight. Are you hanging in there?"

"I'm okay," she assured her Krav Maga instructor.

"You should come back to the studio."

"Maybe next week," she hedged.

"When you're ready. You'll get there."

She smiled at his confidence, wishing she shared it.

As she and Connelly walked home, she swung

her hand in his. She was sleepy from gin and the long week. She plucked her phone from her handbag to text Jordana and let her know that they were on their way. That's when she noticed a blizzard of missed calls and texts from Will and Naya. The most recent text had come in only a half an hour earlier from Naya, copying Will:

I know it's late but the three of us have to talk. Are you around this weekend?

Sasha texted back and suggested meeting in the office in the morning. She wondered idly what had them worked up. It couldn't be too important because neither of them had left a message.

She imagined they wanted to tell her that Kevin had responded to their deadline. If she met with them in person, maybe she could convince them to look at the bathtub crayons. She pushed the texts from her mind and turned her attention to Connelly. They traded stories about their friends for the rest of the short walk home.

They tiptoed inside, and Sasha went upstairs to check on the sleeping twins while Connelly drove Jordana home. As Sasha turned to leave the nursery, her eyes fell on the linen bin that held the blocks Finn had cut his teeth on. Her conversation with Maisy came rushing back. She grabbed the bin and the unicorn play set next to it and snuck out of the nursery with them. Next she headed to the playroom.

She was sitting on the floor, with the skirt of her black and white dress spread out around her, surrounded by boxes and bags of toys, puzzles, and games when Connelly returned.

"What's going on in here?" he asked in a loud whisper.

"Sorting some toys."

"I thought you already took out all the Playtime Toys stuff."

"I did."

"So what's this?"

She looked up at him. "None of this can stay out until we confirm it's safe."

"Sasha, you're tired. It's been a long week—"

"No. Connelly, this is important. I have to go into the office tomorrow and meet with Will and Naya. You have to promise me you won't let the kids play with any of these toys until I'm sure it's okay."

He gave her a long, searching look.

She preempted him before he could say anything. "Listen, I know what you're thinking." He gave her an *'oh, yeah?'* look.

She went on, "You're thinking I'm being a control freak. I don't have work to keep me busy, and I'm worried about Prachi, so I'm channeling all my anxiety toward the kids. You think I'm over-reacting to a minor risk. How'd I do?"

"Pretty dead on," he admitted.

"And you might be right about all of it. But why don't you just humor me for a couple days?"

"Easy enough for you to say. You're not the one who's going to be trapped in the house with two kids who aren't allowed to play with any of their toys."

"You can be inventive. I'm sure you'll think of something."

"Oh, I can definitely be inventive," he countered.

She smiled and held out her hand. He helped her up from the floor to her feet.

30

Will and Naya were waiting in the conference room when Sasha walked into the office on Saturday morning. It was always a little bit strange to be in the offices when the firm wasn't officially open for business—the empty workstations; the quiet computers; the dim light. It all made the firm feel alien and wrong, not like her second home. Today the sensation was especially disconcerting because she felt unwelcome, like an outsider.

She tried to shake the feeling as she pushed open the door to the conference room. Naya and Will beamed at her with twin smiles.

"Look," Naya said, pointing at the table. "Will

stopped at Presto George's and got espresso and biscotti."

She looked down at the treats and back to their faces. "What's the occasion?"

"Good news," Will answered.

She walked across the room and helped herself to a cup of espresso and a crunchy slice of biscotti. "I'm all ears."

"Yesterday, Steve Harold agreed to drop his case. I have a written statement from Kevin Marcus affirming that they are not going to file the draft complaint and that the firm is ending its representation of Mr. Harold. In the letter, Kevin also extends a personal apology."

He extended a sheet of paper. She juggled her cookie and coffee in her left hand and took the one-page letter in her right. She scanned it. As Will noted, the letter set out Steve Harold's agreement not to file the draft complaint; the fact that Prescott & Talbott would not be representing him going forward, and a carefully worded lawyer apology. Marcus's letter also stated that there would be no point in her suing Steve Harold because he was judgment-proof.

Something about the short letter wasn't sitting right with her, but she couldn't pinpoint the problem. Besides, Will and Naya were watching her expectantly, with barely controlled excitement. So she placed the letter from Marcus on the table in front of her and looked back at them.

"Great. But couldn't you have just emailed me a copy of the letter?"

"There's more," Naya said, giving Will a *'get on with it, already'* look.

Will cleared his throat. "Naya and I discussed it, and despite the malpractice carrier's reticence, we think you should come back to work."

"Wait. Why is the carrier hesitant? I thought the issue was the Harold lawsuit?"

Will bobbed his head from side to side. "Well, yes and no. They did suggest that you might want to wait until you complete the Accelerated Rehabilitative Diversion program. But we need you here."

"I see," Sasha said slowly, not sure how she was feeling.

"We let the folks at Recreation Group know that you'll be returning. They're beyond thrilled, even though they know you won't have an active role in the arbitration until you finish your anger management course."

His words triggered a wave of conflicting

emotions within her. First, she felt relief that her exile was over, followed by excitement at the thought of returning to her legal practice, and then, finally, the smallest hesitation whispered in her ear.

"Mac, what's going through your head right now?" Naya asked in a quiet voice.

Sasha sat silent for a long time. Her heart thumped. When she spoke, she said the only thing she could. "I'm not ready to come back."

Will knitted his eyebrows together. "Pardon?"

Naya shook her head vigorously, and her gold hoop earrings swung wildly from side to side. "What do you mean, you're not coming back? This is your firm."

"I know, but I can't. I have a moral obligation to stop Playtime Toys. You'd never guess how I spent my night last night—I boxed up all the twins' toys and took them out of the playroom. I'm *afraid* to let them play."

"Sasha—" Will began.

But she was on a roll. "I've always thought that if I did my research and bought from companies I trusted, my kids would be safe. There are thousands and thousands of pages of regulations designed to protect families like mine, but if a company like Playtime Toys is motivated to circumvent them, they're not worth the paper they're printed on. The kids are in danger, and their parents don't even know it. I just can't let that go, but if I come back I can't try to stop it."

"Nobody's asking you to look the other way, Mac," Naya broke in.

"But if I come back, I'll have to look the other way. Because even if Recreation Group waived the positional conflict, after the sale goes through, there'd be a direct and actual conflict of interest. So, I'm not coming back—at least not now." She took a shaky breath.

Naya rubbed her temples. Will worked his jaw.

"Do you have *any* actual information?" Will finally asked. "Or is this all still your gut."

"I'm pretty sure the Artie the Aardvark bathtub crayon set failed its heavy metal testing. But I don't know how to confirm it."

Naya walked over to the long, low credenza that ran along the entire front wall of the conference room. It was lined with four-inch thick, black binders. Each binder was stuffed with due diligence documents from the Playtime Toys review.

She flipped wordlessly through several binders until she found what she was looking for. She carried the open binder to the gleaming walnut table and dropped it with a thud.

"Look," she said, pointing to a line in a chart of products. "This is the most recent product chart they've provided—you know, in lieu of an actual searchable database."

Sasha and Will leaned over the document, their heads nearly touching.

Sasha followed Naya's brightly polished fingernail along the row labeled 'AR462.' She read aloud: "Artie the Aardvark crayon set; MSRP, $4.99; category, art supplies; test results, N/A."

"N/A?" Will echoed. "Not available?"

Naya shook her head. Her mouth was a tight line. "Not applicable. Art supplies are exempt from the testing."

Sasha furrowed her brow. "Who in their right mind would classify bathtub crayons as an art supply? It doesn't make sense."

"But if they weren't classified as a toy, they wouldn't have been tested. So they couldn't have failed the test," Will pointed out. "It looks like you got bad information."

No way, she thought. There was no other explanation for those crayons to be in Prachi's oven. They had to have been the product she wanted to retest.

Think.

Naya and Will were watching her. She looked at Naya. "When did they send this chart over?"

"Beginning of the week. I had Caroline date stamp it." She pointed to the upper right-hand corner.

"Do you have the one it replaces?"

Naya nodded and flipped to the next tab. "I just moved it back in the binder. I didn't want to take anything out, not with the arbitration hearing pending."

The three of them crowded around the page again. Sasha's heart raced as she read the entries for AR462 to herself: Artie the Aardvark crayon set; MSRP, $4.99; category, bath toys; test results, passed.

She raised her head and looked at Will. He was staring at Naya.

After a silence that seemed to stretch into the next week, Naya exhaled, "Let's call the client."

Hofstott's Café Monaco
Oakmont, PA

WILL PULLED some strings and secured a lunch reservation for five on short notice. The white-tablecloth Italian restaurant was hardly convenient to their Shadyside office, but it was just around the corner from Ned Klein's Oakmont mansion. And when a lawyer was summoning the president and the general counsel of a client into a meeting on a Saturday afternoon it generally paid to be accommodating.

Parker Rivers, Recreation Group's in-house counsel, had the farthest drive of any of them, coming all the way from her Upper St. Clair house. But Parker was a fairly young attorney to have landed a plum general counsel position and she knew it. So when she came tripping into the restaurant slightly out of breath, she was all apologies. "I'm so sorry I'm late. I had to get the kids to soccer first."

"No worries," Will assured her. "We're grateful you and Ned were able to take the time away from your families to meet with us."

"How are Chase and Hunter?" Sasha asked Parker as the other woman took the empty seat. After she'd left Prescott & Talbott, Sasha hadn't kept up with many of the associates she'd supervised, but Parker had faithfully sent Sasha a Christmas card every year—even after she herself had left to take the job at Recreation Group. As a result, Sasha'd seen the metamorphosis as Parker's children had grown from chubby-faced babies to gangly kids.

Parker smiled. "They're good. And the twins?"

"Keeping us busy," Sasha said.

The pleasantries out of the way, Sasha gave Will a meaningful look.

He let his gaze travel around the table and said, "We asked you to come to lunch because we have a situation."

Ned's pleasant smile vanished. "What kind of situation?

Will gestured to Sasha. "Sasha, the floor is yours."

She pinned her eyes on Ned. He was the one who mattered. Parker would fall into line behind him.

"You retained us to advise you on the acquisition of Playtime Toys. And we know your decision to go ahead with the transaction was based, at least in part, on the opinion letter we gave you after we completed our due diligence review. At this point, our firm can no longer stand behind that opinion." She dropped her bombshell and flicked her eyes to Parker.

The color drained from Parker's face. Sasha knew Parker was tallying up the legal fees her department had already incurred in vetting the company and pursuing the arbitration. Across the table, Ned was likely doing his own set of calculations about stock pricing and bonuses.

Ned frowned. "Because they're dragging their feet about getting the database to us? I thought you all said we could work that out in the arbitration."

Naya caught her eye and gave her the slightest nod of encouragement.

Sasha took a sip of her ice water. Then she continued, "No, not because of the database. Look, Ned, if I can speak frankly, one of the things I most admire about your company is your commitment to your mission and your values."

Ned smiled.

She plowed ahead, "That's why I know you

don't want to do business with a morally bankrupt company. And, unfortunately, that's what Playtime Toys is."

"I don't understand." He looked to his in-house attorney for help, but Parker turned up her palms in a 'beats me' gesture.

"Bear with me while I walk you through this, because it gets somewhat convoluted. As you know, they missed their deadline for turning over the completed product database. Apparently, that's because they hadn't actually created the frame-work. All they had was a stack of papers. So they found a scientist in India with dual degrees in chemistry and computer programming and brought her over on a skilled worker visa to create the database and get it up and running. Her name is Prachi Agarwal. Have either of you heard that name before?"

Ned shook his head no.

"Not that I can recall," Parker said.

"Okay, so Dr. Agarwal was the architect for the database and she was solely responsible for popu-lating it," Sasha summarized.

"They have one person populating the data-base?" Ned exclaimed. "No wonder they're so far behind schedule. It's data entry—a team of temp workers would have it done in a week."

"They *had* one person. But Prachi Agarwal's been missing since Monday. The police are investigating her disappearance. Foul play may be involved."

Parker's blue eyes were enormous. "What's going on? Is her disappearance somehow related to her work for Playtime Toys?"

Sasha paused as a team of wait staff arrived at the table with warm rolls and a pitcher of ice water. After they'd taken salad and appetizer orders and were too far away from the table to hear the conversation, she continued, "To answer your question, Parker, I think it might be. This seems like a tangent, but it's not—as you know, I was recently involved in an altercation."

Ned nodded. "Right. That's why you chose to step down from the arbitration team."

"As part of my agreement with the district attorney's office, I'm taking an anger management class. Prachi Agarwal is—or was—one of my classmates."

"Really?" Parker asked.

"Really. When I spoke to her at our first

session, I didn't know where she worked, but she told me she was being set up by her company because she'd alerted management to a safety issue."

"A safety issue? With a product?" Ned wondered.

Naya spoke up, "We have a guess, but it's not confirmed because they haven't disclosed the problem as part of their supplemental document productions."

"Not only have they not disclosed it to you; they also haven't disclosed it under the consumer product safety law. They haven't undertaken the requisite re-testing of the product. They haven't initiated a voluntary recall," Will added.

"All they've done is covered it up and smeared the reputation of the woman who brought it to their attention," Sasha said. "Now, Dr. Agarwal wasn't about to let the issue go, so she apparently planned to retest the product herself. But then she vanished."

"What's the product?" Ned pressed.

"Well, the police found three samples of the Artie the Aardvark Bathtub Crayon Set in her apartment."

Parker made a disapproving sound. "Kids get those bathtub crayons all over their naked, little bodies, not to mention their mouths. If they're toxic ..."

She trailed off, and Sasha let the silence blanket the table for a minute. Then she moved in for the kill.

"Right. And based on documents they *have* produced in the arbitration, sometime in the last week or so, they updated their product schedule to recategorize the bathtub crayons. Now they're listed as an art supply, not a toy."

"What's the difference?" Ned asked.

Sasha knew his general counsel could field this one. "Parker?"

Her eyes flashed. "It's a big difference. If the product's a toy, they have to test it for the heavy metals. But if it's an art supply, not marketed to children under the age of fourteen, they don't."

"Oh, come on. I've seen those crayons in stores. There's a freaking cartoon aardvark on the package." Ned thumped the table in outrage. The clattering of silverware drew a few looks from the wait staff.

"Precisely," Will said. "If Playtime Toys is

willing to do something this egregious to save a few dollars, what else have they done? That's why we can't stand behind our opinion any longer. We're sorry."

The table fell silent. Then Naya said, "We're recommending that we enlarge the arbitration to cover a claim that they haven't been fulsome in their disclosure. We'll ask for supplemental documents, basically redo the diligence. It'll mean a delay, but you have to be sure about what kind of company you're buying."

Sasha added, "Take a day or two to think about it, but you have to decide soon."

Ned shook his head. "There's nothing to think about. The Consumer Product Safety Improvement Act exists for a reason. The regulations are onerous for a purpose. They protect Parker's kids and Sasha's kids, my grandkids—we're talking about getting cute with a product category to weasel out of compliance and for what? A bigger profit. At the expense of the wellbeing of *children*. That's gross." He jabbed his finger angrily in the air, pointing around the table as he spoke.

He took a breath and went on. "I don't need an expanded document review and a new opinion. I wouldn't take that company now if it was offered for pennies on the dollar. Parker and I will break the news to the board. You folks do what you need to in order to rescind the purchase agreement and nail their hides to the wall. Can we stop them from shipping the bathtub crayons?"

"I think so," Sasha ventured.

"In that case, let's order some vino and toast to taking them down," Ned boomed.

The tension that had been hanging over the table dissipated. Even Will cracked a smile.

Sasha shook her head. "No. You and Parker should celebrate dodging this bullet, so go ahead and order. But the rest of us have a long weekend of work ahead. So I'll take a rain check on the celebration and stick with water."

Naya turned to her with a half-smile. "I thought you weren't ready to come back?"

Sasha grinned at her. "Oh, I'm back, baby."

LEO and the twins had just finished lunch when his cell phone rang. He checked the display.

"Mommy's calling from her office. Do you want to say hi to her?"

Finn and Fiona looked up from the pile of cardboard boxes that surrounded them. Finn shook his head no. "We're busy, Daddy," Fiona told him.

He chuckled as he answered the call. "Hey."

"I just wanted to see how you're doing. By my calculation, this must be Hour Seven of the no toy regime," Sasha said.

He laughed again. "As it turns out, they've been so busy they haven't even noticed that all of their toys are gone. We made homemade play-dough this morning. Then they spent well over an hour in the backyard making a fairy house out of rocks and sticks. After lunch, they raided the pile of boxes in the recycling and have been making trains, forts, and what may or may not be a rocket. So I guess saving our children from potential, horrific poisoning wasn't such a bad idea after all."

"Glad to hear it," she said. "Especially because it looks like it's going to be a late night for me."

"Does that mean you're back in business?"

"Yep. I'm back, and now Naya, Will, and I are going to try to save everybody else's children from potential, horrific poisoning."

He could actually hear the smile in her voice.

"Go get 'em, tiger. I'll hold down the fort. And the rocket. And whatever else these two create."

She laughed. "Don't wait for me for dinner. But I'll be home in time to tuck them in."

31

Sasha woke early and took the twins to the playground while Connelly slept in. She figured it was the least she could do because, with her parents out of town, the weekly Sunday dinner with the McCandless clan was canceled. That meant he'd be two-on-one with the twins for the second full day while she was at the office.

After a solid hour of swinging, running, and sliding with Finn and Fiona, she got them their breakfast before gently shaking Connelly awake and handing him a mug of coffee. Then she jammed a baseball cap over her unwashed hair, laced up her shoes, and ran to the office, hoping the exercise would jolt her brain into working mode.

She popped her head into Will's office to say a quick hello. He was already busy pulling relevant caselaw from the online databases. She wondered when Will Volmer had last done his own legal research and made a wager with herself that it hadn't been in this millennium.

She then spent the morning wrapping her arms around the Consumer Product Safety Improvement Act of 2008 and the federal regulations interpreting the act. Dense was one way to describe them. Mind-boggling also worked. She stopped only to refill her coffee mug and stretch her back.

By ten-thirty when Naya arrived, straight from church in her Sunday best, the Code of Federal Regulations' tiny print was swimming in front of Sasha's eyes. She worked for another half an hour before her blurring vision convinced her it was time to take a break.

She rousted Naya and Will from their offices so they could all gather in the conference room for a status update.

"How are you guys doing?" she asked, as they trudged into the room like zombies.

"Wired and tired," Naya told her.

"I've finished drafting the legal argument," Will announced. "And it's a good thing because I'm afraid I'm going to need to duck out for a few hours this afternoon."

"And where do you think you're going, mister?" Naya teased.

Will looked sheepish. "My wife called and reminded me we have a previously scheduled social obligation. A First Communion party for Kevin Marcus's youngest daughter, Cassidy. I won't stay long."

Leave it to Will to hobnob with the man who'd just threatened to sue her and their firm, Sasha thought in wonder. A second thought struck her. "Can you casually ask Kevin a question for me? Without ruining the mood or anything?"

"That depends on the question," he countered.

"How was it that Prescott & Talbott came to represent someone like Steve Harold? Something's been niggling at me ever since I read Kevin's letter. If Steve Harold is so broke that he's judgment-proof, how on earth could he afford Kevin's hourly rate?"

Will's eyebrows shot up his forehead. "Now,

that's a darn good question. I'd like to know the answer to it myself."

"Good," Sasha said. "Now you can sneak away to your country club party with a clear conscience."

"How's your section of the argument coming, Mac?" Naya asked.

"I've got the statutory language laid out and I'm just about finished sketching out the regulatory provisions that we need to be sure to include," Sasha said. "How's the statement of facts look?"

"Solid," Naya told her. "The two versions of that schedule of products is the key. That and the packaging from the Artie the Aardvark bath set ought to be enough to get an injunction."

Sasha beamed. She felt the familiar exhausted but energized sensation that came from a big litigation push. "Awesome. Let's try to get the whole shebang together before we leave today. Then tomorrow morning, we can all read it over one last time with fresh eyes and get it on file. With any luck, we'll have a hearing on Tuesday."

"We have to have a hearing on Tuesday," Naya informed her in a suddenly grim voice. "Playtime Toys sends out its shipments every Wednesday. The bath crayons will be on their way to store shelves if we don't have an order in hand before then."

Sasha's stomach clenched. "Good," she deadpanned. "I've been thinking all that's missing is a ticking clock."

"More like a ticking time bomb," Naya muttered in response.

LEO'S CELL phone chirped in his pocket. He grabbed for it and accepted the call before the noise could wake the twins.

"Agent Connelly," he answered.

"Oh, are we being formal tonight? In that case, this is Officer Minet."

"Ha, hi, Cheryl. The call came up as Pittsburgh Police Switchboard, so, better safe than sorry."

"Roger that. Listen, I know it's late but I thought you'd want to know—"

"Did you get a break in the Agarwal case? Did someone ID the sketch?"

"We got a break, I think. But not that. The Little Washington police—"

"Who?"

"Washington County. We just call it Little

Washington, you know, to distinguish it from big Washington—the one in D.C.?"

He'd never heard that particular bit of Pittsburghese before. "Sure. Makes sense. Go ahead. Sorry I interrupted."

"Anyway, they got a tip about some stolen guns. Your ATF boys came down and they conducted a joint raid on a camp, or more of a compound, really, up in the mountains outside Uniontown."

"Did they hit the jackpot?"

"The federal agents hauled away a crate of Smith & Wessons. And, suffering from an apparent failure of imagination, they left everything else for the local PD."

"Such as?"

"Such as a couple five-gallon drums of hydrochloric acid, several vats of lye, a pallet of bottles of bleach, and an array of off-the-shelf enzyme removers for getting out bodily fluid stains. You know, like blood."

"I take it the owner isn't just a clean freak," Leo said drily, trying to tamp down his rising excitement.

Cheryl barked out a laugh. "J.T. Dunmore's a freak, all right. And according to the locals, a tweaker. But he also swears he's just a go-between, a bag man. He holds the goods for the seller, takes the cash from the buyer, skims off his cut, and then passes it on to the seller. I'm sure he steals a little extra from both parties to the transaction along the way, but he's a bit player."

"Useful, though. Because he knows a lot of names," Leo observed.

"Yep. And in a miracle of organization and work ethic, he put together a system to keep track. Names, dates, amounts. Not too shabby. He gave the gun dealer and would-be purchaser to the ATF, and they cut him loose."

"I imagine the local authorities were interested in speaking with Mr. Dunmore."

"Right. Here's where you come in. He sells the cleaning supplies to a guy named Dutch. Apparently, Dutch has a bit of a reputation around town and eyebrows might go up if he bought his own bulk acid and such."

"He's a cleaner?"

"Yeah. I don't know if he's *your* cleaner, but given the state of that apartment ... we're going to have a chat with him in the morning. You want to tag along?"

"Yes."

Sasha would be busy with her request for an

injunction, but he couldn't pass up this opportunity. He'd find someone to watch the kids.

"I'll have a unit pick you up at ten. Don't get too excited, though. It may be a nothingburger."

"I know. And thanks."

She was right; this Dutch character could be a dead end. But, in truth, Leo was pretty sure he wouldn't be. Cleaners—criminals who specialized in removing evidence of a murder—were a rare breed. It was disgusting work. It took a special kind of evil—and an iron stomach. If Dutch hadn't cleaned Prachi's apartment, he would know who had.

32

Leo watched his wife sleep. He almost never woke before her, but when she still wasn't home when he'd gone to bed at midnight, he'd set his phone to vibrate so he could bring her coffee in bed. He sat on the edge of the bed with her coffee mug in his hand and considered letting her sleep in. She'd be furious. But she was knocked out, her arm thrown over her eyes. Dead to the world.

Yes, definitely let her sleep in, he decided.

As he eased himself off the mattress, her eyes popped open and she shot up to a seated position.

"Morning!" she chirped, instantly awake.

"Good morning, sunshine." He handed her the coffee.

She took her first sip. "Thanks. Where are the kids?"

"Playing in their boxes."

"Seriously?"

He nodded. "Yep. How's the brief coming along?"

"It's in good shape. We're going to file it today."

"Does that mean you'll be home for dinner?"

"Yes. But don't get too excited. I have to leave the office to go to anger management. Then I'll come back here for dinner with you and the kids. But after they're in bed, I have to go back into the office to prepare for the hearing."

He frowned. "You're going to wear yourself out. Maybe work from home after dinner?"

"Maybe," she allowed. She drained her mug and said, "What's on your schedule for today?"

"Hank's going to watch the twins for me for a few hours. I'm tagging along on some local police business," he told her.

She blinked. "What?"

"The police officer who checked out Prachi's apartment for us is interviewing a man who may know something about her disappearance."

"Really?"

"Yes. It may be a break. It may be nothing," he

cautioned her much as Minet had cautioned him the night before.

"Wow." She thought for a minute. "Can you ask him if he knows Kevin Marcus?"

He cocked his head at the non sequitur. "Who? Isn't that the Prescott & Talbott partner who was going to sue you?"

"Right. Get this. Yesterday, Will went to a party that Kevin threw."

"Did your invitation get lost in the mail?"

She snorted. "Anyway, Kevin claims that Steve Harold is judgment-proof. So Will asked him how Harold could afford Prescott's fees. Kevin had been hitting the bubbly pretty hard, so he let it slip that Harold hadn't retained him. The person paying the bills was some fraternity brother of Kevin's from college."

Leo didn't like how that sounded. "Did he get a name?"

She shook her head. "Will said Kevin's eyes bugged out of his head as if he realized he'd said too much. Naya's going to try to run down a list of his fraternity brothers from Penn State. But it's really weird, don't you think? Why would someone else pay Steve Harold's legal bills—unless Harold was working for the guy?"

"Right." He thought for a minute. "Listen, keep me posted on what Naya finds out. After we talk to this Dutch character, I'll see if Officer Minet's willing to pay Steve Harold a visit and rattle his cage about his financier."

"You've got yourself a deal," she said. She reached up, wrapped her arms around his neck, and nuzzled into him for a few seconds.

He took her empty mug from the bedside table. "Refill?"

"What kind of question is that?"

He laughed. "Fair enough. You want me to bring it up here?"

"No, I'll be down in a bit. I'm going to take a quick shower."

THE CRISIS MANAGEMENT consultant could hear Steve Harold banging around, shuffling papers, and softly cursing on the other end of the line. He waited, patient and placid, until Harold's voice sounded in his ear.

"Okay, I found the papers from the district attorney. She was ordered to take an anger management class that meets from six o'clock to seven o'clock at the Community Probation Office in East Liberty. You want the address?"

"No." He didn't need it. He'd already looked on-line. The office was within walking distance of Prachi Agarwal's apartment. The smart money said that's where the two women had met.

"Okay ... so, then are you done with me?" Harold asked tentatively.

More than you know, the consultant thought. What he said was, "One more thing. The attorneys have closed out your case. You don't have to worry about your past coming back to haunt you."

"That's a load off my mind," Harold babbled. "Thank you. Thank you so much."

The consultant hung up without responding. He didn't have time for niceties. He had somewhere to be.

33

Leo watched Eric "Dutch" Price squirm—
or attempt to squirm—in his seat. But
Dutch was a large man. And he was
squeezed into a standard-issue chair, which left
little room for squirming.

Cheryl Minet loomed over him as best she
could given his bulk. "I don't have time for games,
Mr. Price. Somebody sanitized an apartment over
in Bloomfield last week. Whoever did it was a pro.
I've heard you do good cleaning, but not that good.
We were just hoping you'd know whose work it
was."

Leo tried to keep his skepticism off his face.
There was no way Dutch Price was going to fall for

such blatant reverse psychology. *What was Cheryl's end game?*

The mountain shrugged its shoulders. "Dunno what you're talking about."

Cheryl went on, unperturbed. "I mean, they were almost pro. Whoever it was did screw up one thing."

"Really?" Dutch said in a tone that suggested he didn't care at all about the answer.

"Really. And, no, it wasn't leaving the note. We know that was intentional. He overlooked something else."

Dutch's expression might as well have been carved out of granite for all the reaction he showed. Then his eyes flicked away from her and over to Leo, who was sitting quietly in the corner. It was just a nanosecond, but it was a flash of pure fear.

Got him.

"Oh, yeah? I think you're BSing," Dutch countered.

Cheryl Minet shrugged. "You can think what you want." She turned and grinned at Leo out of Dutch's line of sight. "I guess I didn't introduce my friend, did I?"

"Who—the pretty boy in the corner?" Dutch jerked his head toward Leo.

Leo unfolded his long legs and rose from the chair. He walked across the room and stood directly over Dutch, forcing the seated man to tilt his head back to meet his eyes. "I'm a cleaner of sorts myself. I work for the federal government for an agency you've never heard of. An agency that doesn't even officially exist. And Officer Minet's right. Whoever cleaned that apartment was thorough, but careless."

Dutch stared at him with pebbles for eyes.

"He forgot to check the oven," Leo whispered it in Dutch's ear as if it were a sweet nothing and Dutch were his lover.

Dutch was a statue. He made no movement, no sound. But he swallowed just a little too hard.

Leo turned and walked toward the door. Minet made as if to follow.

"Wait—"

They turned to face Dutch. "What was in the oven?"

Cheryl Minet smiled. "Children's bathtub crayons."

Dutch furrowed his brow. "Crayons? Are you freaking kidding me? Who cares about some dumb crayons? Not that I was there—because, like I said, I wasn't."

Minet's frosty smile vanished. "Think hard, Dutch. Just try not to strain your brain. Do bathtub crayons belong in the oven? You have a fifty/fifty shot of getting this right. Good luck."

He glared at her.

"I'll take that as a 'no.' Why would they be in the oven, you might ask yourself. And, if you were smart, you'd say because she wasn't supposed to have them. Now don't you worry your little pea-brain about the details. Just know they're relevant to our investigation. Very relevant."

He made a face that suggested he was unconvinced, but Leo could see him faltering. He glanced over at Minet. He didn't know her well, but he'd seen her in action long enough to know that she wouldn't be above a little completely legal subterfuge.

He leaned against the wall and gave Dutch a long, slow, smile. "We've got a police artist working on a sketch with a resident of that apartment building. Remember the guy walking his dog? Well, he remembers you. It makes sense. You *are* a distinctive-looking gentleman."

"Sure, right," Dutch scoffed, but his voice was wobbly.

"You want to take your chances, Eric? That's fine by me," Minet trilled over her shoulder. "Once the sketch artist finishes up, I won't need you. Between the witness identification and J.T. Dunmore, you'll go down for Prachi Agarwal's murder."

Dutch's nostrils flared. "I don't do wet work. Strictly clean up."

"Doesn't matter to me. If I can pin the murder on you, I can close the case. What do I care?" Minet shot back.

"Tick tock, Dutch," Leo added.

The big man shook his head. "The guy who hired me, they call him the Knitter. He's weird. Like really weird."

"The Knitter? What is this—a *Batman* comic?" Minet asked with a sneer.

"I don't know his name," Dutch protested. "Nobody does."

"Does he pay cash?" Leo asked.

"Usually."

"How's he contact you?"

"Cell phone. I'm sure it's a burner, though. Are we gonna deal?" Dutch asked again.

"You're going to have to give us something more than a comic book supervillain who pays cash and uses an untraceable phone before I drag an ADA down here," Minet told him.

Dutch huffed and thought and thought and huffed. Finally, "He's a fixer. But he calls himself a ... uh ... corporate crisis management consultant. Works exclusively for companies. No personal matters."

Minet looked at Leo as if to say *'is that enough?'*

Leo shrugged.

"Okay, Dutch. You cool your heels. I'll call the district attorney's office. Maybe do some scales to warm up your throat. It's time to sing."

SASHA WAS STARING at the wall, trying to slow her racing brain, when her telephone rang. Just minutes earlier, she'd signed the motion and supporting brief and had passed them along to Naya and Caroline to get them on file with the court.

She looked at the telephone number scrolling across the display. Connelly.

She punched the button to answer the call

before the receptionist could grab it. "Can you talk?"

"Your timing couldn't be any better. I'm literally doing nothing. Naya's getting the papers filed now."

"I only have a few minutes, but I want to fill you in on what happened this morning when we interviewed that guy," Connelly said, his words coming out in a rush.

"Did he know anything?"

"He did." He paused. "I'm sorry, Sasha— Prachi's dead. This man, Dutch Price, disposed of her body."

Sasha's chest turned to cement. She squeezed out a breath. "How'd she die?"

"I don't know. He doesn't know. He wasn't there when she was killed; he was hired by a man he calls the Knitter to clean up the mess."

Sasha wrinkled her nose. "What did he do with her body?" she asked, even though she wasn't sure she wanted to know.

"It was pretty gruesome," he said in a raw voice. "He basically liquefied her. Let's not talk about it now."

"Okay," she said softly. After a beat, she asked, "What happens now?"

"The police will track down her next of kin in India and notify them."

"What about this Price guy?"

"He's talking. He's spilling details on several cold cases, but he's still going away for a long time. He's got too much blood on his hands."

"Did he give you the Knitter? And why is he called the Knitter?"

"Price says he doesn't know the man's real name—and he was introduced to him as the Knitter, so he's got no insight into the nickname. But what he does know concerns me. This Knitter calls himself a corporate crisis management consultant."

"A consultant?" she echoed.

"Right. And apparently he specializes in fixing problems for companies. I think you're right that the scene with Steve Harold and the bar was a set up. Playtime Toys must have hired this Knitter to take care of its problems meeting its deadline."

"Sonofa ... so instead of fixing their bad product and putting money into the database, what? They decide to just silence Prachi? And to cause a delay, they messed with my career? What kind of business does that?" She shook with anger.

"A dirty one. I know you're mad. But listen, you have to be careful until we find this guy."

"Do the police have any leads?"

"No. Officer Minet wanted to go rattle some cages at Playtime Toys, but I'd rather not tip them off that we're onto them if we can avoid it. I suggested we go get Steve Harold and put some pressure on him—see if he gives up the Knitter."

"Is she listening to you? I mean, you don't have any jurisdiction, do you?" Even after three-and-a-half years of marriage, she was foggy on the details of what her husband actually did for the government. It was better that way.

"No. For now, she's happy to coordinate with me. I dropped a plum in her lap. When I go to get the twins from Hank, I'll talk to him about making our involvement more official. This Knitter sounds like someone who should be on someone's radar within the organization."

"What about the police artist's sketch—did Officer Minet show it to this Dutch person?"

"She did. He said it resembled the Knitter, but it wasn't a lock. The problem is he's a fairly innocuous, middle-aged, upper-middle-class white man with no distinguishing marks. Hell, I'd bet half the partners at your old firm would be a match for this sketch."

"Hey, that reminds me. Remember how Naya was going to try to track down Kevin Marcus's fraternity brothers? Somehow—don't ask me how —she got her hands on a Penn State yearbook from the 1970s. There's a group picture of Kevin's fraternity, captioned with names and everything. Maybe the guy who paid Steve Harold's legal fees is in the picture. If Harold IDs him, maybe *he* can lead the police to the Knitter."

"Or he is the Knitter," Connelly said matter of factly.

She must be tired, she thought. Because that elegantly simple possibility had escaped her. "Oh, right. Or that. Anyway, do you want us to send over the picture?"

"Definitely. Hang on."

She heard a muffled exchange between him and someone else in the room—presumably Officer Minet. Then he was back on the line, rattling off a fax number. "Ask Naya to send it right over, okay? We'll show it to Dutch and then take it with us when we go to get Harold."

"A fax? What year is it there—1998?"

"I'm sure it's an e-fax. Let's focus, shall we?"

"Sorry. My brain is fried." She laughed at her own denseness.

"You need to get some sleep tonight," he told her in a voice laden with concern.

"I will."

"In the meantime, please be careful. If this Knitter dude was hired to neutralize you, there's no reason to think he's not going to keep trying."

That woke her up like a glass of ice water down her back. "Great."

"Don't worry. Minet's going to try to get approval to send a black and white to sit outside the building."

She swallowed a laugh. It was a fundamental difference between them that he thought the prospect of being surveilled by law enforcement was comforting, not creepy. "Okay."

"I gotta go. I love you."

"Love you more. Kiss the babies for me—and tell Hank thanks for taking them today."

"Intra-agency child care benefit," he cracked.

She hung up, ripped the sheet of paper with the fax number from her notepad, and headed for Naya's office. She bumped into Naya in the hallway.

"I was just coming to see you," Sasha said.

"*I* was coming to see *you*," Naya responded. "The request to enjoin Playtime Toys from selling the bathtub crayons was accepted at 2:24 p.m. and assigned to Judge Zarelli."

"Don't know her. Do you?"

"Nope. But our hearing's tomorrow at one thirty. So I guess we'll get to know her together."

"Great. Thanks for taking ownership of getting it done. Can you come to Will's office with me for minute? I need to tell you both something."

Naya threw her a questioning look but said, "Sure."

They headed toward the end of the hall. Sasha paused at Caroline's workstation. "Is he in there?" Sasha asked.

"Yes." Caroline answered without looking up from her typing. "Go ahead in. I don't mean to be rude; I'm just trying to catch up. He had me working on his inserts to your brief all day."

Sasha smiled to herself. Will may have joined the twenty-first century by doing his own legal research, but it sounded like he was still dictating his briefs.

She peeked through his open door. "Can Naya and I come in for a second?"

He waved them in. "Of course. Do we have a brief on file?"

"We certainly do. It's been assigned to Judge Zarelli for a hearing tomorrow," Naya said.

"Good draw. She's very fair—and laidback, for a federal judge. What time?"

"One-thirty."

He nodded and steepled his fingers in thought. "We should all call it a night early and get some rest. Sleep is as important as any other preparation."

Sasha nodded. There was a time when she'd have laughed off that advice and pulled an all-nighter. But that time was many briefs ago.

"Agreed," she said. "But first, I need to talk to both of you. I have an update on Prachi Agarwal."

Will looked over the top of his reading glasses. "Oh?"

"Connelly is with the Pittsburgh police. They went to interview a man who they thought might know something about her disappearance." There was no good way to say the next part, so she just said it. "She's dead. She was killed."

Naya gave her a careful look. "Does that mean they've got the guy who did it?"

"No, afraid not. They got the guy who disposed

of her body. He claims he was hired by someone who calls himself the Knitter. He fixes corporate problems."

"You mean corporate problems like not being able to deliver a database on the agreed date?" Naya asked, pulling a face.

"Probably that kind of corporate problem," Sasha agreed.

"And one way a person might propose fixing such a problem could be to set up the other party's attorney on a criminal charge to divert everyone's attention from the deadline," Will posited.

"It's not outside the realm of possibility. And, when that failed, Prescott threatened to sue me civilly."

Naya said what they were all thinking. "So, they tried to silence Prachi Agarwal and failed— now she's dead. They've tried to silence you and failed ..."

A long silence followed.

"Right," Sasha said in a resolute tone. "Let's not panic. The police are on it. They're going to go interview Steve Harold to see if he can give them anything on this Knitter person." She handed Naya the paper on which she'd written the fax number. "They'd like you to send them the picture of Kevin Marcus and his fraternity brothers."

Will jerked his head. "Surely you don't think Kevin's wrapped up in this? Granted, taking on the representation was in poor judgment, but ..."

Sasha chose her words with care. "I think he probably represented Steve Harold as a favor for a fraternity brother, and that's the extent of his involvement. But maybe that fraternity brother is connected to the Knitter. There've been too many coincidences."

He sighed. "I suppose that's true."

She went on, "The police officer who's working with Connelly put in a request for a squad car to park in front of the office. But we should probably all be a little extra careful until they find this guy." She didn't want to scare them, but she did want them to be vigilant.

Naya nodded, wide-eyed. "Let me go send this picture to Leo so the cops can get this guy off the street." Naya folded the sheet of paper into fourths and left.

Sasha trudged back to her office to highlight the statutory provisions she wanted to commit to memory before the hearing. She'd have a copy of the full statute with her, and the motion and brief cited the relevant portions, but judges were human beings. And human beings tended to trust people who sounded like they knew what they were talking about. Being conversant—or even better, fluent—with the Consumer Product Safety Improvement Act was the first step in convincing Judge Zarelli that she was right about the need for an injunction. Once they had an injunction, Naya could start the not-so-fun process of blowing up the deal.

She stared dully down at the words, wishing she had time to take a walk and recharge her brain. She checked the time. No walk. She had to wrap this up before it was time to leave for her anger management class. She couldn't afford to take a breather. She plunged back into her reading.

She was so intent that, when Will rapped on the frame of her open door ninety minutes later, the noise startled her. She jerked her head toward the doorway. "I'm sorry. I wasn't trying to sneak up on you."

"You didn't. I was just concentrating," she reassured him as she capped her pen. "Do you need something?"

"I'm getting ready to leave for the day. Naya and I thought we'd walk out together. Are you going home soon? We've had a long couple days. You should get some rest. Besides, you shouldn't be here alone."

"I'll be leaving in a bit. I'm going straight to anger management."

He frowned at her answer. "I don't think—"

"Will, I'll be fine. Honestly."

He held her gaze for a long moment. Then he exhaled. "Of course. And I know you're well equipped to protect yourself. But, given your current situation ... well, here." He crossed the room to hand her a printout of a case.

"Is this for the argument?"

"No. It may be relevant to your personal situation."

She tilted her head and gave him a puzzled look.

"Read it," he urged her.

"Um, sure. I'll review it tonight. Thanks" She slipped it into the outside pocket of her bag.

"Get some rest," he reminded her.

"Have a good night," she answered absently, her mind already back on her argument.

34

The crisis management consultant was standing under the awning of a shuttered corner market across the street from the probation center office when he saw Sasha McCandless-Connelly striding purposefully toward the building. She walked like a woman who wanted to communicate she wasn't easily intimidated and had places to be.

He lowered his head but followed her into the building with his eyes. As she disappeared inside, his cell phone rang. It was Charles Merriman.

"Yes," he answered in a clipped tone.

"The sale may be blowing up. Sasha McCandless-Connelly just filed papers in federal court asking a judge to prevent us from shipping our products out this week. She claims it could cause irreversible harm to the public, as well as financial harm to her client, if our shipment goes out." Merriman's voice shook with rage or worry or panic.

Probably a combination of all three, the consultant decided.

"That's troubling," he empathized in an effort to calm the client while he came up with a solution.

"I thought she was out on leave."

"Evidently, she decided to cut it short. Given—"

"Evidently," Merriman snapped.

"Don't interrupt."

"I'm sorry."

"As I was saying, given that our efforts to neutralize her haven't had any lasting success, I recommend a more permanent solution."

"Permanent? No, no, that's not necessary. We've reached out to Ned and his team at Recreation Group. We're going to meet with them at their offices tomorrow morning to try to work out a business resolution that obviates the need for a hearing in federal court. It's a long shot, but maybe we can even salvage the deal," Merriman stammered.

Business people, the consultant thought in disgust. "None of the measures we've taken have stopped her from interfering with your deal. She's a human cockroach—an arrest didn't stop her; being on probation hasn't stopped her; the threat of civil litigation and the loss of her livelihood hasn't stopped her. You may want to have her eliminated."

"Have her *eliminated?*" Merriman echoed, scrambling to create a meaning for the word other than its plain meaning.

"Correct, eliminated." He didn't have time to dance around while his client feigned struggling with a moral quandary.

"If you're suggesting what I think you're suggesting, absolutely not."

"It's your decision, of course. I'll just note that a dead lawyer can't make any arguments—winning or losing."

"And then what? She's just one lawyer. Recreation Group will hire another one. Are you going to kill them all?" Merriman sounded disgusted.

The consultant stifled a laugh. Here was a man who was willing to falsify or circumvent federally required test results to ship an unsafe children's product to the market; a man who was comfortable with trumping up an employment infraction to intimidate a would-be whistleblower into silence or risk the loss of her visa; and, it must be said, a man who had hired him to make his problems go away however he saw fit, so long as the company and its leadership didn't have to get their hands dirty. This particular moral high ground was built of quicksand.

Now and then, in his line of work, the consultant had to gently coax his clients to the correct conclusion, gradually over time. But time was a luxury they didn't have in this particular instance.

"It's your company. And it's your problem," he said bluntly. "I have no doubt that my proposed solution *will* silence her. If you decide to implement it, you know how to reach me. If not, good luck tomorrow."

"I didn't call to ask you to ... you know. I called to see if you had any idea how Sasha McCandless-Connelly could have learned that there's a problem with our product. Prachi Agarwal's the only one who knew." Merriman's tone was accusatory.

A dark, seething anger took hold of the consultant. *That's* how the two women were connected. They'd met at their anger management class, and somehow the lawyer had pried the information out of the scientist. He punched his fist into his thigh.

"I have some idea," he answered through clenched teeth, staring hard at the door to the probation office.

"Well, if you've been sloppy, it's cost us quite a lot," Merriman shot back. "I expect a refund."

"Don't hold your breath. If Prachi Agarwal confided in Sasha McCandless-Connelly, it wasn't as a result of my work. I don't have time for this nonsense. Goodbye, Charles."

"Wait!"

"Yes?" Perhaps Merriman had worked through his moral dilemma after all.

"Dr. Agarwal—she wasn't eliminated, was she?"

The consultant didn't respond. He ended the call and leaned back into the shadows to wait for the attorney.

THE SUN WAS low in the sky but hadn't yet set when Sasha walked out of the community probation office with Lani. She waved goodbye to the girl, who sulked into the passenger seat of a car that sat idling under the 'No Parking' sign with its blinkers flashing.

Out of curiosity, she craned her neck to get a glimpse of Lani's foster mother. Then she hurried to the corner and crossed the street. She walked with purpose. Outwardly, she looked like a person who was alert and aware of her environment. But, in truth, it was window dressing, illusory. Her over-tired mind had been wandering all day, she was raw and rattled by the news of Prachi's death, and she felt wrung out and overwrought after having spent an hour grappling with her emotions under the watchful eye of Karen Hogan. She needed to eat one of Connelly's home-cooked meals, listen to her children's laughter, take a long hot shower, and collapse into bed. She'd be fresh and ready to gear up for the hearing when the sun rose.

Busy planning out her night, it took her longer than it ordinarily would've to realize someone had fallen into lockstep with her on the other side of the street. She glanced over and spotted an unassuming-looking guy in a nice suit. Probably just another urban commuter on his way home, she tried to assure herself.

But something about the way that his

measured step matched hers so precisely planted a seed of unease in her stomach. She veered sharply and ducked into Trader Joe's parking lot, just as she was about to walk past it. She glanced over. The man was on the other side of the traffic circle, and cars were flowing by.

She darted into the grocery store and grabbed an arm basket. Although she didn't need anything in the store, putting some distance between herself and the man immediately alleviated her anxiety. She was probably being paranoid about the man, but now that she was here she might as well pick up a few things. She wandered up and down the tight aisles, tossing dark chocolate-covered pretzels and almond-stuffed olives into the basket. She ended up in the dairy aisle, so she picked up a glass quart of milk even though she didn't know whether they were running low or well supplied with Fiona's favorite beverage. On a whim, she picked out some avocados.

There's a reason Connelly does the shopping, she thought, as she stood rapt, surveying the granola section. Tropical fruit and ancient grains or dark chocolate and berry? Motion at the end of the aisle interrupted her nut-and-grain-based reverie. She jerked her head away from the granola display just in time to see a white guy in an expensive suit turn the corner.

Her anxiety came rushing back. *He's not the only white guy in a suit in Shadyside*, she told herself. But there was no reasoning with the pit of her stomach. She hurried to the front of the store, using the racks of fresh-baked bread to shield her from his view. She peered at him through the whole-grain rolls.

No, that was her white guy in a suit. She recognized his gait. And now that she was getting a closer look at him, she recognized his face, too. But from where? She couldn't think. Not with the way her heart was thudding in her chest and her pulse was thrumming in her ear.

Keep it together. It's still light. You're two blocks from home.

She raced to the express register and started piling her random assortment of food on the conveyor. She smiled tightly at the chattering cashier, peeled off two twenties, and left without waiting for her change and receipt.

As she approached the exit, she glanced up at the convex mirror hanging above the doors. She didn't see him behind her. *You lost him*, she assured herself. All the same, she shifted one bag to each hand to balance her load and half-jogged through the parking lot.

STUPID, careless, rookie mistake.

The consultant realized he was shaking with anger at his failure. He couldn't believe he'd allowed her to make him. He should have stayed a pace behind her. He'd been distracted by the call from Merriman, but there was no excuse for incompetence.

He took a breath and reframed the event. Perhaps it was good that she'd seen him. Worrying about who he was and why he was following her could knock her off balance and interfere with her ability to concentrate on the upcoming hearing.

Marginally calmer now, he checked the map on his phone and traced her likely route. When he'd first been contacted by Playtime Toys to deal with their Sasha McCandless-Connelly problem, he'd done comprehensive research into her background, as was his usual practice. She had an unusually high public profile thanks to her propensity for getting into trouble, but finding her home address had been a challenge. Apparently after some long-lost relative had tracked them down, she and her husband had made arrangements to remove that information from the Internet. But, like anything else, it remained available—for a price.

Despite having paid a tidy sum to acquire her home address, he hadn't yet paid her a visit. He'd viewed the information as his ace in the hole and, frankly, assumed she'd be more vulnerable at her office than at home.

Given her grocery store visit, however, she was clearly headed home, not back to work. He doubted he'd have access to her once she was inside her house, but it was worth taking a look. He set off toward the McCandless-Connelly residence as darkness fell.

When he reached her street, he circled the block and walked along a narrow, bumpily-paved alley behind her house. He didn't stop, but slowed his pace, as he strolled by her back fence. Two tricycles in the backyard. A wooden playhouse. An iconic red wagon, its handle resting against the trunk of a leafy tree. A retriever burying a stick. The sound of music floating through an open kitchen window. He noted it all and filed it away for later.

35

Leo eyed the random assortment of groceries that Sasha dumped on the kitchen counter. "I didn't know you were stopping at the store. I'd have asked you to pick up a bunch of cilantro."

She turned from the refrigerator, still clutching the wholly unnecessary milk she was trying to shoehorn into a spot. "Do you want me to run back out?"

"Nah. I improvised. You have just about enough time to change before dinner if you want to get out of your work clothes."

"Or I could set the table," she offered.

"That's what the minions are for."

She laughed and disappeared upstairs to

change while his miniature kitchen staff rushed in to help with setting the table. He sincerely hoped that the unbreakable glass plates she'd found at some cafeteria supply store were, in fact, unbreakable. *Only one way to find out,* he figured.

After dinner, which was the usual organized chaos of two new-to-utensils eaters and a dog who was smart enough to lurk under the table for falling food, they tucked the twins into bed and headed into the kitchen to clean up. It was her turn to pick the music, so he just tuned out the soundtrack to whatever musical was playing. She hummed along and sang softly as she rinsed dishes and loaded the dishwasher.

"How'd it go with Steve Harold?" she asked over her shoulder.

By unspoken agreement, they hadn't talked about the Knitter or Dutch or anything related to Prachi's death during dinner. He imagined she'd been bursting with questions. Unfortunately, he had no good answers.

"Harold's in the wind," he told her.

"Hiding?"

"Either hiding, dead, or drunk somewhere. Nobody at his apartment complex has seen him. The ex-wife gave us a list of bars to try. The police will check them tonight, but for now, he's unreachable."

"You don't really think he's dead, do you?"

He grimaced, wishing he hadn't raised the specter of another death, but, having done so, he had to see it through. "We'd be foolish not to consider it as a possibility. I suspect he's not. And I really hope they smoke him out fast because Officer Minet was told there's no protective detail for you without some direct connection between Prachi Agarwal's death and Steve Harold. We need him to identify the Knitter."

She nodded grimly and resumed loading the dishwasher. He tried to keep his focus on the leftovers he was ladling into a storage container and loading into the refrigerator. She was arranging the dirty dishes all wrong. He knew he should wait until she left the room and try to quietly reorganize them as he usually did. For some reason, tonight he just couldn't ignore it.

He joined her at the sink. "Hey, you know, if you put all the silverware in the basket facing the same way sometimes it doesn't get completely clean. But, if you alternate forks and spoons and put some of them upside down, they won't stick together."

She turned her head slowly to pierce him with a look. "Did you just critique my dishwasher loading?"

His tone had been mild—jovial, even. Hers was … not. He took a closer look at the dark half-circles under her eyes and forgot about her lousy dishwasher-Jenga skills. He rubbed her shoulder. "Why don't you hit the sack? I'll finish up here."

She smiled up at him. "I didn't mean to rip your head off—even if you are a bit of a freak about things. I'm just …"

"Tired?" he supplied helpfully.

"Agitated. I had a crappy day. We've got the hearing tomorrow afternoon, which we're scrambling to get ready for. We need to focus. But while I was in my class, I got an email from Naya. Our client agreed to meet with the CEO of Playtime Toys in the morning."

"What's the point?"

"I assume it's a last-ditch effort to work something out before the hearing. It's futile, but this deal means a lot to Naya. So, we're going to leave Will to handle all the last-minute hearing prep, and she and I will waste a morning at Recreation Group's office hearing what Playtime Toys has to say." She rolled her eyes.

"Could it be a deliberate attempt to prevent you from presenting your best case at the hearing? You know, spread you thin?"

"Could be. But their lawyers should be there, too, so it'll hurt them just as much. I doubt it's malicious, it's just stupid. And, then to cap off my lousy day, some weirdo followed me from the probation office."

The community probation office, designed to provide a convenient location for services for people on probation, was not in the best section of the neighborhood. He frowned. "Panhandler? Pervert? What kind of weirdo?"

"Neither. This guy stuck out because he was clean, well-dressed, affluent looking. I feel like I've seen him around before. But he gave off a definite sketchy vibe. That's actually why I stopped at the grocery store—to shake him."

He stared at her for a long moment.

"What?"

He stared some more.

"I did lose him, though. Don't worry."

He shook his head but continued to look at her stone-faced, waiting for her to catch on. He knew the exact second she did because she went wide-eyed and pale.

"You think it was the Knitter?"

"Or somebody working for him."

She usually wasn't this clueless—in fact, she usually wasn't clueless at all. He wondered just how much strain the bar fight and its consequences had caused her. He reached into his pocket and pulled out a copy of the police artist's sketch. He unfolded it and smoothed the sheet flat on the kitchen island.

"Did he look like this guy?"

She leaned in front of him and studied the drawing. "That's him," she said almost instantly and with conviction.

It was good enough for Leo. His wife had a frighteningly accurate memory. He nodded. "I'll call Minet." He moved toward the doorway.

"Wait." Sasha plucked at his sleeve.

"What?"

"Two things. One, I have seen him before."

"Where?"

"In Jake's, the day I got in the bar fight. He was there when I called Maisy."

"Are you sure?"

"Positive. He was a little too attentive to me, watching me. I thought he was just a creep."

"What's the second thing?"

"Tell Officer Minet there's probably security camera footage at Trader Joe's."

He crossed the room and kissed her. "You're brilliant."

When he lifted his head, he looked through the kitchen window. He swore he caught a flash of color and motion just outside the gate. He squinted and waited. Maybe it was just his eyes playing tricks. Then Mocha trotted to the back-door and let out an urgent whine.

"What's the matter, boy? Do you need to go outside?" Sasha asked the dog.

Leo squeezed her shoulders. "Check the locks then go upstairs to the kids' room."

"Connelly—"

"There's someone in the alley. Go."

She ran to the door and rattled the knob to make sure it was locked. Then she raced to the front of the house to check the front door. He bolted up the stairs to unlock his gun safe.

SASHA PICKED Finn's sock monkey up from the floor beside his bed and tucked it under his arm. He moaned, tightened his grip around Monkey, and sighed in his sleep. She smoothed Fiona's sweaty curls away from her forehead. Fiona didn't stir.

She stood watching them for a moment, and then she went to the window and tried to pull it up. Locked. She pressed her head against the pane and stared down into the backyard. Connelly must have turned on the spotlights. The toys and bikes scattered across the yard were transformed into vaguely sinister lumps in the shadows cast by the light. She took one more look at the sleeping twins. Then she tiptoed out of the room and down the stairs, avoiding the step with the squeaky board.

The front porch lights were on. The living room lights were on. The dining room chandelier was on, its dozens of little light bulbs casting little shadows on the wall. The kitchen was dark, except for the dim light cast by the sole bulb in the vent over the stove.

Connelly had dragged a chair to the big window in the breakfast nook and was staring out into the night, his Glock in hand. Coffee was brewing.

"Kids still asleep?" he asked without taking his eyes from the window.

"Yep." She picked up her briefcase and dragged

the other chair over to the breakfast nook, bringing it to a rest beside him.

"You don't have to keep me company. You should get some sleep."

He was right. She should get some sleep. But there was a zero point zero percent chance she was going to fall asleep while her husband was up all night guzzling coffee and playing sentry.

"I'm just going to read over some materials for tomorrow," she told him. "And I can fetch your coffee for you so you don't have to leave the window."

He shifted his eyes slightly and looked at her. Whatever he saw in her face apparently convinced him not to argue. "Okay."

She settled in next to him. "Did you call Officer Minet?"

"Yes. Still no sign of Harold. But the computer folks digitally aged that yearbook picture to see which fraternity brother, if any, is a match for the police sketch."

"And?"

"And the Knitter appears to be a man named Brady Linghold. They're trying to find out everything they can about him. I told Minet to let me have a crack. Hank's working on it right now. I also told her Mr. Linghold may be in the neighbor-hood. She's going to have a unit do patrols all night. They're also pulling the security camera video from the grocery store."

"So, in the meantime, you're going to stare into the backyard with a loaded gun?"

"Yes."

"Sounds like a plan. Aren't the motion detec-tors on?" She wasn't sure why the floodlights were still ablaze.

"I switched them off. I want the lights on all night. I want him to feel as though he's going to be spotted the second he sets foot on our property."

"It could have been a dog or a squirrel or some-thing that you saw," she said.

"Could've been. Wasn't."

She bit back her response. Instead, she got two mugs down from the cabinet and poured them each a cup of coffee. Connelly took his wordlessly. She sipped hers as she sorted through her hearing papers. A sheet of paper peeking out from the front pocket of her bag jarred her memory.

She set aside her CPSIA argument and reached for the case Will had given her. She almost did a spit take with her coffee when she realized what the case was about. It was an old

Pennsylvania Supreme Court decision collecting self-defense cases and discussing the elements required to establish the imminent peril defense. She read it, scribbling notes in the margins. Then she dug a highlighter out of her bag and read it again, more slowly.

36

The crisis management consultant shrank back against the neighbor's garage door and blinked into the light that seemed to pour from every window of Sasha McCandless-Connelly's home—every room on the first floor was lit up, with the exception of the kitchen. Then the outside lights blazed to life; the sudden blast of brightness was disconcerting. He stood and watched for a while, certain that he was also being watched from within. They knew—or feared—that someone was out here.

If he'd believed in luck, which he did not, he'd have been convinced that his was souring. Ever since he'd taken on the assignment for Playtime Toys and Charles Merriman, he'd been beset by a string of misfortune. It was time to cut ties with old Charles, he mused. Asking for a refund had been just the beginning, he suspected. Next would be a veiled threat to go to the authorities. And then— who knew?

The attorney could wait. He'd deal with her another day. He slinked around the corner and crept to the end of the alleyway. Then he strolled out onto the sidewalk with his hands in his pockets, nice and slow. Just a guy out taking his after-dinner walk.

37

Sasha greeted Connelly with a fresh mug of coffee as he stepped out of the shower and wrapped a towel around his waist. He waved the drink away.

"No thanks. My stomach is already bathed in pure acid from our all-night caffeine bender. It's all yours."

She smiled gratefully and sipped at the blessed beverage. The night had passed slowly, but uneventfully. She could use all the coffee she could guzzle. "Any word from Hank?"

"Brady Linghold, also known as the Knitter, was a fair-to-middling business student at Penn State. In his junior year, he was busted for running a gambling ring out of his girlfriend's dorm room."

"Not the fraternity house?"

"I'm sure more level-headed brothers would have shut that down. They could have lost their charter for that sort of thing. Anyway, he was sentenced to community service and anger management—because he apparently took a swing at the arresting officer. In the course of the program, he learned how to crochet and knit as a way of controlling his temper. Hence, the nickname."

"I don't think it worked," Sasha deadpanned.

He chuckled. Then he narrowed his eyes and gave her a curious look. "Are you learning any fiber arts?"

"No. I'm learning to count to ten and focus on my breathing."

"Hey, just like Fiona."

She mimed kicking him in the shin. "Anything else?"

"He's been involved in loads of financially questionable transactions. Our forensic financial guys are going to talk with his bank in the Caymans. I also talked to Officer Minet. She's going to head out to Playtime Toys to chat with the CEO and see if she can confirm that he hired Linghold. Presumably, he'll lawyer up, but you never know."

"Probably. Listen, can you ask Minet to hold off on her visit to Playtime Toys? Charles Merriman, the CEO, is meeting with us at Recreation Group this morning, remember?"

Connelly frowned. "This is now a murder investigation. It's not really the sort of thing you put on the back burner."

She gave him a look. "It's important to Naya that we blow up the deal as professionally as possible. This matters to her. Merriman's not going anywhere. And it's not like he's personally running around killing people."

He huffed. "I'll talk to Cheryl."

"Thanks." She headed for the closet to pick out a dress and jacket to wear to court.

He trailed behind, still talking, "And, last but not least, a patrol officer found Steve Harold in a bar on the South Side just before last call. Once he sobers up, they're going to push on him pretty hard to get him to give up Linghold. I really want to be there, but given the circumstances—the bar fight and all—the district attorney thinks it's cleaner if I'm not."

"It is," she confirmed.

She slipped on a light blue sheath dress and its matching suit jacket. "So what are you going to do today? You can't hang out here."

"I'm sure I could handle anyone who shows up, but ..."

"The kids."

"Right."

"Could you go to Hank's place? Together, the two of you could fend off a small military unit."

"We probably could."

"But I guess we really can't risk endangering his family," she said, rethinking.

He nodded. "That's sort of where I came out on it, too. I'd really like to tag along with Minet when she interviews Merriman if I can find someone to watch the kids. Are your parents still out of town?"

"Until Wednesday. But if you're really worried about the Knitter, my parents' place would be a bad choice anyway. Their idea of home security is leaving the spare key under the same flowerpot that it's been under since I was in second grade." She thought for a moment. "Daniel and Chris have a doorman. Nobody gets into that building unannounced. Unless Chris has a piano student in for a lesson, he's usually pretty free during the day."

"What about their furniture of death?" Connelly countered.

"As between furniture of death and actual murderer, I think sharp edges would be the lesser of the two evils. The bigger problem will be the fact that Daniel ignores the 'no juice' rule."

Connelly flexed his biceps. "Don't worry. The enforcer will be there. You put your face on. I'll call Daniel."

"Okay, but if you do run out with Minet and leave them with Chris and Daniel, tell them I mean it. No juice for the twins. It's not good for them."

He nodded solemnly. "No juice. I promise, so long as you make me a promise."

"What is it?"

"I want you to drop us off and take the SUV. Don't walk anywhere, okay? Until we find this guy, we're on high alert."

She waited a beat for his obligatory jab at her over the fact that her car was in the shop following a collision with a parking garage column that jumped out at her. But it didn't come.

"No walking," she agreed, trying to pretend the jitters in her stomach were related to her upcoming court appearance only.

38

"Yes?" Charles Merriman's voice shook.

The consultant was pleased to hear the quaver of fear. "I've reconsidered. I'd like to meet to talk about the refund you requested."

"Really?" Audible relief oozed from Merriman. Then, suspicion. "We don't need to meet. Just reverse the wire."

"It's not that simple." Although, of course, it was that simple. And Merriman likely knew as much. The consultant coughed. "We need to discuss the strings that would be attached to the return of the funds."

"The ... strings?" Merriman echoed, his indignation evident.

"Yes, strings. You're complicit in anything unfortunate, shall we say, that may have happened. It's important that you understand that if I go down, you're coming with me." As he spoke, he ran his fingertip along the point of his blade in a gentle motion, almost a caress. He drew just a drop of his own blood.

"I'm not going to dignify that with a response," Merriman huffed.

"Ten o'clock. We'll meet at the coffee shop across the road from your fish and chips restaurant."

"No, I can't. I told you—I'm meeting with Recreation Group this morning. Right at ten, as it happens."

"Hmm. Do I have your word that you'll maintain your silence about my work for you?"

"Yes, of course. It goes without saying," Merriman said eagerly.

"Good."

"Does that mean you're going to give me back my money?"

"I'll see to it that you get what you're due, Charles." The consultant smiled to himself.

He ended the call and checked the time. He'd

plan to arrive at Recreation Group's offices by a quarter past ten. He didn't expect the meeting would last more than an hour.

39

Sasha eased the SUV into a spot between a Suburban and a pickup truck in the parking garage attached to Recreation Group's suburban Wexford campus. She was pleased to see that Cranberry Township was somewhat more generous about sizing its parking spots than was Downtown Pittsburgh. Connelly would never let her live it down if she scratched his vehicle.

She grabbed her bag, took one last swig from her travel mug of coffee, and headed for the stairwell. As she clattered down the stairs, one hand on the metal railing, she checked her messages with her other. Nothing worth breaking her neck over. She slid the phone into her bag.

She trotted across the building's colorful lobby. She always enjoyed visiting Recreation Group's offices. Between the life-sized, live action game pieces and the rainbow-colored statues from children's books, it was impossible not to be cheerful and lighthearted while there. Or, as it turned out, nearly impossible. She was currently feeling stressed, edgy, and flustered—and the presence of a sculpture of a pig wearing a tutu and a tiara did nothing to lift her mood.

"Good morning, Ms. McCandless-Connelly," the security guard said as she scribbled her name in the visitors' log. She noted that both Naya and Charles Merriman had already signed in. She didn't see the names of any of Playtime Toys' attorneys on the list. For a heart-stopping moment, she wondered if Connelly had been right after all. Was the meeting nothing more than a ruse to distract them from their preparation for the hearing?

Great. Well, at least they'd had the foresight to leave Will back at the office. He'd prepared for a hearing or two in the course of his career. He and Caroline would make sure they were ready to go if it came to it. There was no point worrying about it now—they just needed to get the meeting over with and move forward.

She took the stairs to the conference room by twos and hurried down the hallway. When she rushed into the room, four pairs of eyes swung to the door: Naya, Ned, Parker, and Charles Merriman looked up at her from their seats around the table.

"Good morning. Am I late?" she asked as she hurled herself into the empty chair next to Parker. Ned sat flanked by Parker and Naya.

"Good morning," Ned responded. "You're right on time."

"Hi, Sasha. Now that the gang's all here, why don't we get started?" Parker suggested.

"Your lawyers aren't joining us?" Sasha directed the question to Charles Merriman.

He shook his head and blinked at her. "No. I didn't see the need to continue to run up the legal bills, given the situation."

Sasha shot Naya a look. Parker caught it, too, and arched an eyebrow in agreement. Merriman was showing his hand. He was capitulating. The fact that Playtime Toys would throw in the towel wasn't exactly a surprise, but to walk into a meeting with no plan to negotiate was the act of a desperate man—or a distracted one, Sasha corrected herself. Merriman probably had much bigger problems looming on his horizon than the fact that a multimillion dollar deal was falling apart. Problems like a homicide investigation; a massive toy recall, fines, and penalties; and a criminal mastermind who had the goods on him.

Naya leaned across the table. "Mr. Merriman, are you sure you don't want to at least loop one of your lawyers in by speakerphone?"

He looked around the table. "I appreciate the concern, ladies. But let's be frank, shall we? This motion you filed to stop us from shipping our product, that's the opening salvo, is it not? Ned, do you want to buy us or not?"

Ned lifted his shoulders and let them drop as he whooshed out a great breath. He turned to Merriman. "Since we're being frank, Charles, no, we don't. Our company's built on a handful of beliefs that we thought Playtime Toys shared. As we've gotten deeper and deeper into this transaction, it's clear our values don't align the way we thought they did."

Merriman's face reddened. Sasha thought he might argue the point, but he simply nodded. "Then, let's skip the blame and recriminations and work out a way to unwind the deal."

Parker glanced at Naya, who cleared her throat.

"Mr. Merriman, if you recall, the purchase agreement addresses this. If you'll turn to Section 14, subhead—"

The CEO interrupted Naya. "I know you lawyers have drafted section after section dealing with every contingency, but I just want to work out a quick, business resolution. Ned, let's just walk away. I won't hold your feet to the fire about the breakup fee, and you withdraw your motion. We withdraw our arbitration papers. Then we part ways."

Naya blinked rapidly. "Breakup fee? Mr. Merriman, Recreation Group is pulling out of the deal for cause. Multiple causes, actually. Under the circumstances, the breakup fee provision isn't triggered."

"Says you," Merriman responded placidly. "But I'm confident I can find a law firm that will argue otherwise. We can drag this out—it will be an expensive distraction for both of us."

It suddenly was crystal clear why Merriman's lawyers weren't in the room. They'd probably refused to take this tack in the negotiations.

Ned whispered to Parker. She scribbled a note on her legal pad and pushed it toward Sasha. It read: *Ned says fine. Let's just be done with him. Thoughts?*

Sasha tamped down her initial response and spoke in a neutral voice. "Mr. Merriman, will you excuse us for a moment? We'd like to talk over your proposal in private."

"Certainly." He pushed back his chair and stood. "I'll just borrow the room next door and check in with my office. Okay, Ned?"

"Make yourself at home," Ned responded.

Merriman nodded and crossed the room. After he closed the door behind him, they waited several beats in silence. Ned spoke first.

"Can we just agree to walk away?" he asked Naya.

"You can. You shouldn't," she advised. "By rights, they should indemnify you for the costs you've incurred. They haven't proceeded in good faith. They lied, covered up, and Lord knows what else, during the due diligence review and the arbitration."

"I just want to be done with them. I want to move forward," Ned explained.

Sasha looked at Parker. "Parker?"

She hesitated, twirling a strand of shiny blond hair. "It's a lot of money, Ned. We've spent upwards of three hundred thousand dollars putting this deal together."

He shook his head. "I don't care. I don't want to ever have to see Charles Merriman's face after today. That alone is worth a couple hundred grand."

Must be nice, Sasha thought.

"Ned? One issue we haven't discussed is what happens with the bath crayons if you agree to walk away. If you withdraw the motion for an injunction, he could ship those out tomorrow. They'll be on store shelves."

Ned frowned. "Can't the court still stop him? In the public good?"

"It's complicated, but no. We had standing to file the motion because your company could be harmed if they shipped. If you aren't buying Playtime Toys, there's no harm to Recreation Group. They could sell razor blade whistles and you wouldn't be harmed."

"Knowing Merriman they probably *would* sell razor blade whistles," Parker muttered.

Ned shook his head. "That can't be right."

"It's right. We could re-file with a different plaintiff. A concerned parent, for example. We could report them to the Consumer Product Safety

Commission for violating the standards. The CPSC would investigate, possibly impose fines, order a recall, and/or pursue civil and criminal penalties. All of that could happen. But it would take time," Sasha told him.

"It would be cleaner if you got him to agree not to ship the product," Naya said. "As a condition of walking away."

Ned nodded. "Let's do it."

Parker went to fetch Merriman. While they waited, Naya turned to Ned. "I'm sorry the deal fell apart."

He patted her shoulder. "Win some, lose some. We'll find another company to buy. And you'll help us acquire them, won't you?"

"Of course." Naya's face betrayed no emotion, but Sasha could tell she was relieved that Ned wanted to work with her again.

Merriman trailed Parker into the room and clapped his hands together in an oddly jovial gesture. "Well? What do you say?"

"We'll agree to walk away and withdraw the lawsuit if, and only if, you agree not to ship those crayons, Charles," Ned said.

"Nope. That's a non-starter. There's nothing wrong with that product," Merriman insisted.

"If that's the case," Ned pressed, "why did you suddenly change their category from 'toy' to 'art supply'? The only reason you'd have done that was to avoid the heavy metals testing requirement, and we both know it."

Merriman sputtered for a second before he managed a response. "Balderdash. We made a business decision to re-position the product. We feel it's a better fit for the arts and crafts market."

Sasha had heard enough. She opened her bag and yanked out the package of bath crayons. "I stopped at the toy store on McKnight Road on my way here. The *toy store.*" She waved the crayons at him. "Look at this package. This is an anthropomorphic aardvark wearing a beret and an inner-tube ring."

"We plan to rebrand," Merriman said weakly. "New packaging, new focus."

"Charles, please. There are no artists, or hobby artists for that matter, over the age of four in the market for crayons they can use while bathing. You're being absurd," Ned said.

Merriman jutted out his chin. "If you aren't buying us, you have no say in our business strategies—no matter how absurd you might find them."

Ned turned to Naya. "How many pallets of crayons are there waiting to ship?"

She flipped to the schedule. "It looks like six."

"Six pallets. Is that right, Charles?"

"I believe so."

"I'll buy them."

"Pardon?"

"I will buy them," Ned repeated, enunciating each word. He turned to Sasha. "How much did you pay for that package?"

"Four ninety-nine plus tax," she answered.

"I'll pay retail, Charles. Five bucks a package."

"Ned—" Parker began. He held up his hand, and she fell silent.

"What are you going to do with them?" Merriman wanted to know.

"What do you care?" he countered.

Merriman fell silent. Then he said, "You can't resell them."

"I won't."

Sasha watched Merriman's face. He was trapped, and he knew it. If he refused to sell the crayons to Ned, it was tantamount to an admission that they were defective.

Merriman considered all the angles. After a

long moment, he shrugged. Then he stuck out his hand. "You have a deal."

SASHA, Naya, and Charles Merriman all waited for the elevator to the ground floor together in silence. They walked across the lobby to the parking garage elevators together in silence. Naya pushed the button to call the elevator, and then she turned to Sasha.

"Aren't you taking the stairs?" she asked.

Sasha smiled. "No."

Naya squinted at her. "You feeling okay, Mac?"

"Sure thing." She jerked her head toward Merriman, and Naya fell silent.

The elevator car arrived and the doors opened. Merriman stepped back to allow Naya to enter first. Then he turned and gestured to Sasha.

"No, after you," she insisted. She wanted to make sure he got in.

He shrugged and walked into the car. She followed. Naya had already hit the button for the third floor. "What floor do you need, Mr. Merriman?"

"Five, please."

Naya looked at Sasha.

"I'm going to five, too," Sasha said.

Naya pressed the button for the fifth floor as the doors closed. Merriman hummed to himself. As the car rose, Naya turned to Sasha.

"Are you headed back to the office?"

"I am. I'm going to run an errand first, though. Do you want to call Will and let him know the hearing's not going forward or should I?"

"I'll let him know. And I'll call Judge Zarelli's chambers, too," Naya said.

"Great."

The elevator dinged to announce their arrival on the third floor.

"See you later," Naya said as she stepped out into the parking garage.

"Bye."

The doors closed. Merriman kept humming. Sasha jabbed the emergency stop button. The elevator ground to a halt with a jerk. She braced herself for an alarm. None sounded. She exhaled —she'd taken a gamble that the elevator wouldn't be alarmed. Apparently, it had paid off. Or, at least, she corrected herself, it wasn't an *audible* alarm. There was no telling what was happening down at the security station. Better get on with it.

"What the devil—?"

She pierced him with a glare. "I want you to understand this. Ned might be willing to buy up your inventory of mercury-laden crayons and write you off, but I'm going to haunt you until you pay for what you've done—all of it: the unsafe toys, Prachi's death, setting me up in that bar fight. I'm not going to rest until you're in police custody, Mr. Merriman. That's a promise." She pressed the '5' button, and the elevator lurched to a start.

"I don't know what you're talking about," he protested.

"Save it," she said, staring straight ahead. She reminded herself that she was on probation.

40

The consultant was growing restless. He stepped out from his hiding spot between the stairwell and the wall and circled Charles Merriman's white Jaguar. After he'd stretched his legs, he started to walk back to the shadowy corner, rehearsing his plan.

When Merriman appeared, he'd approach the car. Merriman would most likely be surprised, but not alarmed, to see him. He could talk his way into Merriman's vehicle and take care of him. Even if Merriman resisted, though, the consultant was confident he could overpower the CEO. He was soft and complacent.

The *ding* of the elevator door interrupted his planning. He turned toward it as the doors parted.

Charles Merriman stepped out of the car. But he wasn't alone. Sasha McCandless-Connelly stood beside him.

The consultant smiled. *Two for the price of one.* He revised his plan on the fly and reached inside his pocket for his tactical knife.

"Well, this is handy," he said in a conversational tone as he advanced toward them.

"What are you doing here?" Merriman babbled.

SASHA LOCKED eyes with Brady Linghold for several seconds. Then her gaze slid downward. In his right hand, he gripped a wicked-looking knife. The blade, pointed toward the floor, glinted in the dim light. Her heart stuttered.

Not a knife, she thought. Lead pipe, shuriken, nunchucks---she'd happily take her chances. But not a knife. Reflexively, she glanced down at her left arm. Hidden under her suit jacket was a long, ugly scar that ran across her brachial artery—a permanent reminder of her knife fight with a coroner.

And then she laughed softly.

The text of the case Will had given her materialized in her mind's eye, word for word. The first element of a successful imminent peril defense was that the defendant must, in fact, have acted out of an honest, bona fide belief that she was in imminent danger. Check. Second, the belief must have been reasonable in light of the facts as they appeared to her. According to the Pennsylvania Supreme Court, the first element was wholly subjective; the second, entirely objective.

"I wasn't planning to kill you today, too," the man said in a soft voice. "But plans change."

She kept her eyes on the knife. She was pretty sure the death threat objectively satisfied the second element. Saving Merriman's life would weigh in her favor, too, she realized. It would be helpful to have an eyewitness to the attack. And keeping him alive was the only way to ensure he was held accountable for his crimes.

The legal analysis concluded, now all that was left was the actual disarming of her assailant. She judged his distance from them to be approximately eight feet. He appeared to be right-hand dominant.

She glanced at Merriman. He was visibly shaking. She couldn't count on him to help in any way.

She let her briefcase slide from her arm to the ground with a soft thud.

Linghold's eyes flickered down to the bag for a nanosecond then returned to her face.

"Mr. X," Merriman said, the panic rising in his voice, "don't do this."

"Is he serious?" Sasha said to Linghold. "You make him call you *Mister X*?"

"The less my clients know, the better," he told her.

"I guess. But, Mr. X. You could have at least bothered to come up with an alias. Or let them call you the Knitter," she said, keeping her tone conversational as she stepped forward.

He was less than seven feet away now.

Linghold frowned slightly. He quickly smoothed his expression. But it was too late.

"Oh, that's right, Dutch was more than happy to tell the police all about the Knitter. And I don't know for sure that Kevin Marcus rolled over on you, but that's just a matter of time. He hasn't lasted this long at Prescott & Talbott without mastering the art of self-preservation, *Brady*."

"How did you—?" Linghold blurted. Then he caught himself. "No matter."

"Please don't do this," Merriman repeated, his pitch even higher. His voice broke.

Linghold's eyes flashed, and he turned his attention to the blubbering CEO. "Shut up," he said between clenched teeth. "Just be quiet."

While Linghold was occupied with Merriman, Sasha took another step forward.

He turned toward her. "Stop that," he said, jabbing the knife in her direction for emphasis.

Control him. Disarm his. Disable him.

That was the order.

But controlling him meant getting a wrist lock on his knife hand. All well and good in a training environment. A nice way to get her own hand sliced to ribbons in a parking garage.

Okay, forget control. Disarm and disable.

She advanced on Linghold, shouting over her shoulder for Merriman to call for help. Linghold raised his arm to waist level, the knife pointed at her. She didn't run directly at him but slightly to his right, so the knife was between them.

As she closed the distance between them, he slashed the knife through the air.

She sidestepped the blade but instead of grabbing his wrist, she whipped her left hand up, on a diagonal path. She hit the outside of his wrist and chopped the knife out of his grip. The weapon flew to his left, her right and clattered off the hood of Merriman's car.

As his right arm went up and to the side, he instinctively curved inward and covered his groin with his left hand. She'd give credit where it was due. Her plan *had* been to kick him in the groin as hard as she could.

But, as he said, plans change. She grabbed the back of his bent head, wrapping her fingers in his hair, and brought his chin down to meet her knee.

He reached up blindly and raked his fingers through her eyes. Tears immediately streamed from both eyes, making it difficult to see. The pain made it hard to concentrate.

She had no idea where Merriman was or what he was doing, but she fervently hoped the cavalry had been called. And that Merriman had had the good sense to retrieve the knife.

Linghold got his left leg behind her right knee and was forcing her to bend backward. In another moment, she'd be on the ground.

No. No ground fighting, she told herself. *Disable him.*

Bona fide fear, objective under the circumstances, she reminded herself.

She pulled her left elbow back and up as he yanked her down and to the right. Going with the momentum he created, as she turned, she whipped her elbow forward and crushed it into his throat. He rasped and started to collapse backward.

She wriggled free from him and gave him a solid push toward the cinderblock wall behind him. He bashed the back of his head on his way down and slid the rest of the way. Before he hit the ground, the sound of heavy shoes pounding up the stairs echoed through the garage. The stairwell door burst open and a swarm of uniformed officers rushed out, shouting commands.

A familiar six-foot-something, dark-haired, gray-eyed wall of muscle in street clothes beelined toward her. She sagged into Connelly's arms.

"Are you hurt?"

She shook her head. "Just scratches. Where's Merriman?"

"In the back of a squad car, demanding his lawyer."

"How'd you end up here?"

"Hank pulled Merriman's phone records and compared them to Dutch Price's. They both had calls from the same cell phone, which had been purchased with cash in a grocery store in New Orleans. He got the tech gurus to triangulate the calls and voila."

"You mean to tell me the all-powerful Knitter brought his cell phone with him? Pretty rookie mistake."

"No, he didn't. His cell phone is Downtown in his hotel room. But we traced all his calls, and the Uber driver he called this morning was more than happy to tell us where he dropped him off. Does that answer all your questions?" Connelly asked as a fiery female officer who had to be Minet herded a handcuffed, bloodied Linghold toward the stairs.

No, it didn't. She had about a thousand more questions. But they could all wait.

41

Two weeks later

Sasha watched the twins closely. They were splashing in the zero-entry kiddie area of the pool, seemingly oblivious to the foul-mouthed college boys who had just run past and back-flipped into the deep end in a chorus of F-bombs. She was glad Finn and Fiona hadn't noticed, but the behavior was still out of bounds.

No, she told herself. *Leave it alone.*

She glanced at the row of moms in the lounge chairs with their heads bent over their paperbacks and cell phones. Nobody looked up. Across the pool, slightly further into the shallow end, a sweet-looking blonde mom with a big smile caught her eye. Her kids were older than Finn and Fiona, jumping into the two-foot area and chasing after a set of dive sticks amid a flurry of squeals. She'd seen the other woman around the pool but didn't know her name. Now, she gave Sasha a worried, wide-eyed look.

This is not your problem, she reminded herself. She had just closed the chapter on her last Good Samaritan experience. The district attorney's office sprang her early from her anger management class and rescinded her probation after Steve Harold and Charles Merriman gave full statements about Linghold and the plan to set her up in exchange for their respective deals. She didn't need to wade into another situation. Not now; maybe not ever.

The college boys vaulted out of the pool and flung themselves on the chaise lounges closest to the kiddie pool.

"Dude, did you see that the hot lifeguard's working?" A blond, spiky-haired guy said to the darker haired kid next to him.

"You know it." They fist-bumped, and their two friends erupted with laughter followed by another round of F-bombs.

The sweet mom's face went pale and her eyes cut to her two kids who were now watching the teenagers with naked interest.

Ah, crap.

Fiona glanced up at the boys, fascinated. Finn followed her gaze to see where her attention had gone.

Sasha contemplated tossing their swim gear and her bag of sunscreen and snacks into the red wagon, loading up the kids, and pulling them home. But the thought of being chased out of the neighborhood pool by a handful of foul-mouthed teenaged boys didn't sit well with her. She glanced around the pool to see if anyone else—maybe a dad or the pool manager—was going to step in. The rest of the adults were still pretending nothing was happening.

Just then, Connelly came out of nowhere and cannonballed into the pool, splashing up a huge wave to the kids' delight. He cut through the water with perfect form and emerged beside her.

"Hi." He shook his hair, sending droplets of water flying in every direction.

"Hi, yourself. I thought you said you were going to skip the pool and mow the lawn."

"I did say that. But Ken's kid across the street's trying to earn money for a semester abroad. So I paid him twenty bucks to do it instead. Besides, I knew you'd miss my cannonballs."

She smiled. But before she could say anything else, the teenaged boys started hooting and wolf-whistling as the lifeguards rotated stations.

Connelly whipped his head around and gave the teens a death glare. They appeared to be oblivious. Finn was staring at his dad.

"Look," Sasha said in a high voice to draw Finn's attention.

She cranked the handle on the bright orange plastic mill, which made a waterfall of pool water cascade over the side. She had to admit it was pretty cool.

Parker had sent over a whole basket of clever toys from Recreation Group—certified fun *and* CPSIA-compliant, according to the note she'd included—after she'd heard Sasha had removed everything from the playroom. Sasha and Connelly were slowly introducing select toys back into their routine, here and there. But the twins didn't seem to miss them, so they saw no reason to bombard them with playthings.

Now, though, Finn clapped with obvious glee.

"Again!" Fiona demanded.

"Here. You do it." She handed the toy to Fiona and demonstrated turning the crank.

Fiona created a cascade. Finn clapped again. Then he reached out his arms. "My turn."

Fiona scooted across the pool and handed her brother the toy without complaint. She watched with close interest as he turned the handle.

Sasha relaxed almost enough to forget about the teens. She leaned back on her elbows against the pool wall and stretched out her legs in the cool water. Then she heard "look at the rack on *that.*"

She turned in time to see the high-school-aged lifeguard skitter by, her eyes fixed on the ground in front of her.

The other mom started trying to herd her kids out of the pool.

Enough.

"I'm going to set those punks straight," Connelly muttered under his breath.

Yes, let him handle it, she told herself. Then she glanced at Fiona, who was waving bye-bye to the blonde mom's kids. *Was she really going to sit here and model passivity for her daughter—or her son? Like hell she was.*

She put a hand on Connelly's chest. "No. Let me."

He squinted at her face, shielding his eyes from the sun. "Are you sure?"

"Positive."

She exited the pool and wrapped her towel around her waist as if it were a sarong. Then she pushed her sunglasses up to the top of her head and strode toward the four college-aged boys.

They were deeply engaged in an animated conversation about some video of a race car crash that had gone viral on the internet. She walked between their chairs so she was in the middle, with two on either side of her. Water dripped from her legs.

Ignoring her hammering heart, she cleared her throat. "Excuse me."

The guy to her left lifted his head. "What's up?"

"You need to watch your language. There are little kids in the pool."

His buddy elbowed him. "We didn't say anything to any kids."

"No, you didn't. But there's not a sonic wall around you."

A kid from the right leaned in with a sneer. "They can't hear us."

She arched an eyebrow. "They're kids; they're not deaf."

The original speaker bobbed his head. "Yes, ma'am."

The last of them, the one who hadn't yet said a word, followed in a hurry. "We're sorry, ma'am."

She looked from one face to the next, each on the cusp of manhood, each still showing a hint of boy. Then she said, "I appreciate the apology. Now what you need to do is tell that lifeguard you're sorry for what you said about her."

"We're just having fun," the one with the sneer protested.

"She's not here for your entertainment—or to be graded on her appearance. She's here to watch the pool and make sure the swimmers are safe."

Spiky hair rolled his eyes, but all four rose to their feet, grumbling under their breath. They weaved a path around her and trooped over to the lifeguard chair.

She stood, hand on hip, and watched as they offered their apologies with downcast eyes. Only when they trudged back to their chairs, did she return to the shallow end of the pool, shaking with adrenaline.

"Thank you," the blonde mom mouthed.

Sasha nodded; she didn't trust herself to speak just yet.

An older woman marked her page in her book with a finger and gave Sasha an approving nod. "Good for you," she called from her chair in the shade.

Sasha waved at her and sank into the pool between the twins. Connelly wrapped his arm around her shoulder and grinned at her.

The other mom looked over her shoulder and called to her kids, "You guys can have fifteen more minutes."

They whooped with joy and jumped into the pool with big splashes.

The teenagers returned to their chairs and sat for several moments in sullen silence, almost as if they didn't want to let Sasha think she'd run them out. Then they grabbed their towels and headed toward the community game room on the other side of the bathrooms.

"See you later, Pool Mom," the dark-haired one said as they walked by.

"Bye-bye," Finn called to their backs.

"Pool Mom," Connelly mused. "I think it suits you." He leaned down and covered her mouth with a kiss.

Pool Mom. She smiled to herself as she kissed him back. *It did suit her. After all,* she thought, *what kind of world would it be without Pool Moms and Bar Moms and Worried About Mercury in the Toys Moms?*

ALSO BY MELISSA F. MILLER

Want to know when I release a new book?

Go to www.melissafmiller.com to sign up for my email newsletter.

Prefer text alerts? Text BOOKS to 636-303-1088 to receive new release alerts and updates.

The Sasha McCandless Legal Thriller Series

Irreparable Harm

Inadvertent Disclosure

Irretrievably Broken

Indispensable Party

Lovers and Madmen (Novella)

Improper Influence

A Marriage of True Minds (Novella)

Irrevocable Trust

Irrefutable Evidence

A Mingled Yarn (Novella)

Cold Path

The We Sisters Three Romantic Comedic Mysteries

Rosemary's Gravy

Sage of Innocence

Thyme to Live

Lost and Gowned

Wedding Bells & Hoodoo Spells

Wanted Wed or Alive

ABOUT THE AUTHOR

USA Today bestselling author Melissa F. Miller was born in Pittsburgh, Pennsylvania. Although life and love led her to Philadelphia, Baltimore, Washington, D.C., and, ultimately, South Central Pennsylvania, she secretly still considers Pittsburgh home.

In college, she majored in English literature with concentrations in creative writing poetry and medieval literature and was STUNNED, upon graduation, to learn that there's not exactly a job market for such a degree. After working as an editor for several years, she returned to school to earn a law degree. She was that annoying girl who loved class and always raised her hand. She practiced law for fifteen years, including a stint as a clerk for a federal judge, nearly a decade as an attorney at major international law firms, and several years running a two-person law firm with her lawyer husband.

Now, powered by coffee, she writes legal thrillers and homeschools her three children. When she's not writing, and sometimes when she is, Melissa travels around the country in an RV with her husband, her kids, and her cat.

Connect with me:
www.melissafmiller.com

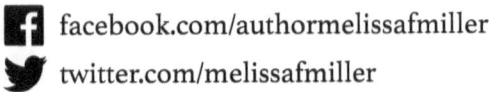

facebook.com/authormelissafmiller
twitter.com/melissafmiller

ACKNOWLEDGMENTS

Many thanks to everyone involved in the production of this book, in particular, my phenomenal editing and design team.